Basketcase

A Classic Tale in Reverse

Sarah J Antoinette

FOR "ADAM"

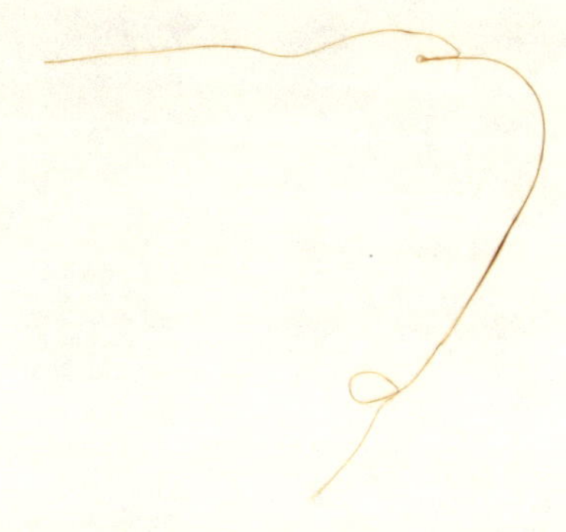

"You own everything that happened to you. Tell your stories. If people wanted you to write warmly about them, they should have behaved better."

-Anne Lamott

From the Author

When I published my first edition of *Basketcase; A Classic Tale in Reverse* in 2016, I had a chip on my shoulder. Olive's story is based on my own, and so writing this book was cathartic, and in many ways, necessary.

Like any other form of therapy, unpacking so much chaos was a messy process. A year after publishing *Basketcase: A Classic Tale in Reverse*, I decided I was no longer happy with the book. Olive was too angry, just as I had been. She needed to step back and regroup with me once more before I let her be the role-model I meant for her to be.

In 2019, I partnered with my rock star editor, Hunter Linar, who worked with me to shape *Basketcase: A Classic Tale in Reverse* into the novel I had envisioned all along. A fajillion thanks to Hunter.

∞ thanks to my friends and family who have been there through the true-life story that inspired this tale and everyone who encouraged me to write it. There are no words to express my gratitude for the support and encouragement I've received throughout writing and publishing (and rewriting and republishing) the story you are about to read.

Sarah J Antoinette

CHAPTER 0

The Land of Sidney: An Island-Nation off the
Western Coast of France

Late 1800s

Olive stared at the prince from across the ballroom. He was tall, strong, and just her type of handsome. As he grabbed his third cookie from the platter she had baked and arranged earlier in the day, Olive blushed.

"Hold my tray, Lionel," she whispered to her brother. "I'm going over there to talk with him."

"Who, Prince Adam?" Lionel asked, organizing the empty glasses and trays at the server's station where they were standing. "Why? I need your help right now."

She turned back to him, annoyed. "You'll be fine without me for a few minutes. Lionel. You've been wanting more front-of-the-house shifts to practice your social skills. Please?"

"You know I still get nervous around this many people, Olive. And the prince? Really? You've heard the rumors. Prince Adam has been known to destroy things when he gets upset. I've heard he threw his cobbler's tools into the fireplace just because one of his shoes pinched. Plus, he probably can only marry a princess."

"The Grimms are an important family! And he wouldn't even have to look beyond Sidney." she faced the ballroom and smoothed back her dark hair. "Cover for me."

"He's going to deny you, waitress! You know that, right?"

She turned back to her brother, lips pursed. "Please don't try and discourage me just because you're not comfortable, Lionel. We are not commoners. We're Grimms. That means something."

"Oh, how could I forget, Your Majesty." Lionel gave a deep bow so that his chest folded over his legs. He grabbed something small from the floor as he did, showing it to Olive with a sly grin. "Somebody dropped one of your handmade hors-d'oeuvres, Princess Grimm."

Her eyes widened. "Don't!"

Lionel chuckled and flung the pastry at his sister. It hit the shoulder of her dress and stuck for a moment before peeling away onto the floor.

Olive scoffed and wiped her shoulder. "Lionel, you bastard! You've gotten gray stuff all over me!"

"That gray stuff is delicious. You should wear it with pride." Lionel covered his face with both hands as he laughed. "Guess you can't talk to the prince now after all, waitress."

Olive sighed, picking up a damp towel from a dishpan underneath the counter. "I've been managing our family's bakery long enough to know how to scrub a food stain clean in record time."

She dabbed the stain with the towel several times before making several short, quick swipes, all in the same direction.

"See, I'm beautiful again!" she teased.

"Now it's just a big wet spot," Lionel pointed out.

Realizing Lionel was right, Olive slipped out of the server's station just as a group of guests cleared out from a nearby table to join the dance floor. She hurried to clear the table of its empty champagne glasses, sneaking a single rose from the centerpiece as she did. Once back behind the counter, she wedged the rose between her shoulder and her apron, wrapping the stem gently around the neck-strap and securing the flower to cover the wet spot where the stain had been.

"I'll have to keep my apron on now, but it makes me look slimmer anyway. Nice try, dear brother." She winked at Lionel and then headed across the ballroom towards the prince.

Prince Adam hadn't moved from where she had first seen him at the dessert table. As she moved towards him, though, embarrassment took hold. Lionel's words had gotten to her after all, and she now felt boring and ordinary.

She was also speechless. Olive hadn't planned anything to say to the prince. With Adam still far enough away for her to turn back if she needed to without him noticing, she paused for a moment, cleared her throat, and tried to imagine what she'd say to a handsome man visiting the bakery.

Prince Adam looked up, spotting her from further away than she'd expected. Olive realized she was gaping at him. He side-eyed her for a moment before gesturing for her to come closer. Still unconvinced that he was looking at her, she glanced from side to side to find that a cluster of dancers was moving in her direction.

"Damnit! Oops, sorry for the—Oh, I didn't even realize," Olive sputtered as she stepped out of the dancers' way. She retreated onto the side of the dance floor nearest Adam.

"Young lady!" the prince called over the piano music playing nearby. "You're supposed to walk *around* the dance floor."

Olive blushed, looking at her feet instead of at the prince who was still a few yards away at the desert table. "I'm aware of that, Your Majesty. Thank you. I'm just a bit tired, is all."

"You're Olive Grimm," he declared, stepping forward.

She looked up. "You know who I am?"

Prince Adam was only an arm's length away from her now, and even more handsome up close. He shrugged. "I know of you, and I've seen you from afar. The Grimm family is an integral part of the progressive dynamic in the Land of Sidney. Your grandfather was an inspiration for the open market. I have orders picked up from your butcher shop and bakery on a regular basis."

"Thank you." Olive nodded first, then shook her head. "But I would remember those orders."

"I use a pseudonym," he explained. "Palace rules."

She glanced at the dessert table where he had been standing, which was behind him now. The tray of cookies was halfway filled with cranberry white-chocolate cookie bars, her holiday-season special.

Prince Adam's eyes followed her stare. "Ah yes. Better Than Christmas Blondies are indeed my favorite, even now that it's springtime. I appreciate you making them by special request all year round."

Olive beamed, stuck somewhere between feeling flattered and floored. She held out her hand to shake his, as if he were one of her ordinary customers. "Well, it's a pleasure to finally meet you, *Ferdinand Holly*. I've been filling your custom bakery orders for quite some time now."

CHAPTER 1
Breaking the Mold, the Mood & the Vase
Six Months Later; Day One

Once upon a gorgeous Autumn day, the type of day that seems only to exist in childhood memories, the Land of Sidney was in full foliage. The air smelled of apple cinnamon and nutmeg, and the trees hung with yellow and orange stars that crinkled with glee in the crisp breeze. Hay bales and dried corn stalks were placed throughout the common grounds of Sidney, creating cove-like nooks where the townspeople could relax between errands.

Prince Adam and his new bride, the royally inexperienced Princess Olive, had made the radical choice to live on their own without the help of servants. They'd spent the morning settling into their brand new home, a Neoclassical style mansion with an impressive set of carved wooden front doors. The mansion sat atop a hill overlooking Sidney and was just a short walk away from the palace.

"It's a modern world, my dear," Adam said, smiling and cornering his new bride in the front foyer. "No dress code, no one to bother us. I can have you how I want you, wherever—and whenever—we want."

Olive squealed and hugged Adam around his neck as he reached around to goose her behind, accidently knocking an empty vase from a stairway pillar. It crashed to the floor, which the couple ignored.

"You can have me anywhere, any time, Prince Adam. You can even have me in our kitchen!"

"And I will, my dear," he declared, kissing his new wife again. "Speaking of kitchens, remind me to show you something once we're done here."

But she didn't care at that moment what he was going to show her. She wanted him right there in the foyer. She wrestled her new husband's arms from around her and sank to her knees in front of him.

Adam leaned his head against the wall and closed his eyes, waiting in anticipation with a confident smirk. Silence fell over the house, but only for a moment before a loud knock resounded through the house.

"What the—!?" Olive sputtered. "Who the hell?"

"Pay them no attention," Adam whispered without opening his eyes. "This is our time."

She smiled up at him and obliged. Silence fell over the house once more.

The knocking at the door started up again.

Olive tried to ignore the noise, but failed. "This is absurd!" she screeched, standing and glaring at the door.

The mood was ruined. The couple did their best to regain composure and make themselves look presentable. With ruffled hair and his shirt halfway tucked back into his breeches. Adam opened the door just enough to stick his head outside. It was the head chef from the palace who had been knocking.

"Well, hello, Mr. Louis!" Adam began. "I can assure you that the new princess is more than capable of cooking us good meals. We won't be needing your assistance today."

Mr. Louis smiled and shook his head, as if he was brushing off what Adam had told him. Nudging the door open with the tip of his foot, he danced his way into the foyer with wide, welcoming arms.

"There's absolutely no need for newlyweds to do their own cooking, Prince Adam. It is simply unacceptable! I'll find my way to the kitchen, and you two can go about your business. Just pretend I'm not even here." Mr. Louis skipped off in the direction of the kitchen, singing to himself.

Through the open front door then walked Mrs. Piper, Mr. Louis's sous-chef, carrying a large basket brimming with food to prepare. Mrs. Piper was short and stocky, the apparent taste-tester of the two.

"Princess!" Mrs. Piper cooed. "It's good to see you two settling in so nicely. I remember when Mr. Piper and I got married. 'Didn't leave the bedroom for three whole days! You're lucky to have Mr. Louis and me to cook for you. Can't let you two go hungry!"

Olive opened her mouth to say something, but Mrs. Piper was already waddling towards the kitchen with the basket of food. Olive sighed. Adam sighed. They looked at each other and rolled their eyes.

"I suppose we can allow it just this once," Olive said, "Let's go back upstairs, dear. Our marital bed is calling."

Once in the bedroom, their frustration turned to passion. The two didn't care that there were people in the house who might hear. Olive began giggling and moaning from the start and was ready to let herself fall apart. She knew she was being quite loud; part of her hoped it would deter the servants from impeding in the future.

"*Princess—!*" came a voice through the open bedroom shutters. "Are you okay? Are you hurt?"

Olive tried to ignore the voice. She became distracted and quiet, however, realizing the voice sounded like a child's, calling up to them from the ground below.

"*Princess!* Are you sick, Miss? Princess! *Princess!*"

The mood was once again lost. Olive collected herself as best as she could, gave Adam a small, apologetic kiss on the cheek, flopped out of bed, and stomped to the open window.

"I'm not hurt, sweetheart!" Olive called down to the young boy. "I was—reading a funny story and laughing myself to tears. How kind of you to check on me."

"Oh my, I'm glad you're okay, then, Princess! Good day to you!" The little boy gave Olive an overzealous wave and a gap-toothed grin before heading back towards the town.

Olive turned back to Adam with forced fire in her eyes. Adam gave her an unconvincing half-smile.

"It's gone, then, isn't it?" she asked.

"For now, it has," he answered. "And I don't like commoners calling on you like that. We need to find a way to keep those people away."

"It's a child, Adam. He was probably out exploring and just happened to come across the house. If we wanted to be isolated from the townspeople, we would have stayed in the palace. This way is better, though. I promise. It's friendlier. You'll learn to love it."

"Townspeople are nothing but a burden while I'm trying to make love to my wife," he huffed.

She huffed back. "Lunch, then?"

He snorted. "Lunch."

Olive didn't bother to put her hair back up. Adam didn't bother to tuck his shirt in. The pair walked down to the dining room, grumpy, and found Mr. Louis and Mrs. Piper joined by a full team of the palace help. At least a dozen busy servants bustled about cooking, cleaning, setting the table, lighting candles, and decorating for Adam and Olive's lunch.

"Be our guests, why don't you," Adam muttered under his breath.

The two sat down at the table with hardly a word to the staff. They didn't eat much, but rather picked and nibbled their way through each of their three courses, annoyed and losing their patience fast.

"More wine, Princess?"

"No, thank you, Miss Annie."

"Your potatoes aren't too cold, are they, Your Highness?"

"No, Mr. Milo, they're just fine." Adam answered.

"I found a broken vase in the front hall, Princess. I cleaned it up for you."

"Thank you, Mrs. Piper."

By the time lunch was cleared, it was already early evening. The prince and princess wanted to be left alone. They needed each other and nothing more.

It was a frustrating task getting everyone out of the house. There was an apparent doubt among the palace staff that Adam and Olive would be able to handle the difficulties of daily life on their own.

"Are you sure you don't need any housekeeping this week, Prince Adam?"

"Yes, I'm sure."

"Princess, you really shouldn't be the one to cook for yourself. It seems so silly when you've got us to do it for you"

"We'll be just fine."

As the couple's aggravation grew, so did the timber of their voices. Each time they spoke, it was louder and louder, until they were shouting.

"How about yard work? Prince Adam, you'll need help with that, won't you?"

"No! Go, now! Leave my wife and I be!"

"Princess, doing your own hair is not as easy as it looks."

"Thank you, Annie, but I've been doing my own hair my entire life! Now please go! We'd like to be left alone!"

"Will you need assistance with—?"

"GO!" the couple shouted in unison.

As the last servant exited, the sun had started to dip behind the horizon. Adam slammed the large double doors that fronted their home and bolted them shut.

Olive looked at the prince with tired eyes. "Now what, dear?"

Adam blushed and cocked his head to the side. "I want to show you something. I wanted to show you much earlier, before we were interrupted. Follow me."

Adam led Olive through the front hall and past a large sitting room next to the kitchen. Beyond the sitting room was a doorway that dropped them into the middle of a long hallway. The hallway split off into two seperate directions, one at a sharp right and the other at a sharp left. Each hallway housed a single door at the very end.

"This way first." He tugged her towards the left

Olive was tense with excitement as Adam led the way. The door at the end of the hall was of carved wood, and he approached it with his chest puffed out with pride. He beamed as he swung open the door, gesturing with his arm for her to enter first.

"Oh, my!" Olive gasped as she saw what was inside: a vast space filled with easels and drawing boards. The walls were filled with books, pens of a hundred varieties, paintbrushes, rulers, paints, and a myriad of other art supplies. The floors were lined with fine, imported carpets and extravagant furniture: large sitting chairs, chaise lounges, and a sofa big enough to seat a large family. There was a desk in the far corner, in front of another large comfortable chair. A row of small, beautiful stained glass windows lined the outer walls above the tall bookcases.

"A library?" asked Olive.

"Almost, my dear. It's my drawing room. I loved designing this house, and it made me realize that I never want to stop creating. This way, I'll always have the space and drive to do so."

"How fantastic!" Olive's eyes sparkled as she looked around the room.

"Since you are a modern woman, dear, I designed most of the house to fit your personality. This room here, though, is much more old-fashioned. Romanesque, if you will." Adam puffed out his chest as he spoke. "I built it to make me feel at home. It's a very similar style to what I grew up with in the palace."

"It's beautiful." Olive beamed.

"How would you like to see the other room, now?" He asked.

Olive nodded her head.

He led her back down the hall, all the way down to the end of the right-hand hallway.

"Close your eyes," he said.

Olive closed her eyes and felt one of Adam's arms wrap around her back, the other holding her hand. She heard the second door open. They stepped inside.

"Now open them!"

She opened her eyes, delighted to see a room just as large as the first. Instead of easels and drawing tables, however, there were countertops and stoves. Instead of books, the shelves held mixers, spoons, measuring cups, and rolling pins. An island counter in the center of the room held a six-burner stovetop and a generous preparation area. Pots and pans of every shape and size hung from a wheel of hooks overhead. Stored underneath the island counter were several large burlap bags labeled flour, cornmeal, and sugar. The main counter was lined with an adorable array of covered containers and bottles, already filled with cooking staples.

The kitchen was similar in size and abundance to the kitchen at Grimm's Bakery, but this one was much homier. The tiles behind the counter were painted with images of things she loved: fruits, plants, musical instruments, and flowers. There were tiles with the moon, the sun, and stars. The cabinets were tall, but simple, and painted a beautiful, mellowing shade of light, dusty green. Floor-to-ceiling glass windows lined the outside wall, stretching upwards into vaulted glass roof overhead. The array of windows let in the amber light of early evening, which lent a shimmery aura to the multicolored rock in the countertops.

"I hand-painted all of the tiles for you," Adam told her. "And I designed this room so you can experiment with all your different baking ideas. You can even leave a mess if you want, and then clean it up whenever you want. Or," he whispered, "you can always just call on a servant to do it."

"Oh, stop it!" Olive laughed, and she jabbed him at the mention of servants. "I love this kitchen more than I've ever loved any other room. I'll love keeping it clean just as much."

"Thank you, my dear. I'm glad you love it. But I do want to reassure you that the servants are *more* than happy to help if we ever should need them."

"I'm sure we won't need them, Adam. I'm beginning to feel worried about all the extra time I'll have now that I'm not at the bakery any longer. My only responsibility as a princess so far has been to plan the royal wedding and be the royal bride. I'm afraid I've never received a clear answer about what I'll be expected to do all day."

"Well, for now—" Adam half-teased as he scooped Olive off her feet, "you can be my newly wedded wife!" He spun her in slow circles around the kitchen, humming a waltz, before setting her on one of the countertops.

Olive smiled and laughed and wrapped her arms around his neck, giving him a long, deep kiss. He had just started to tug at the neckline of her dress, revealing one of her breasts and holding it in his hand.

One of Olive's ears began itching. She tugged one of her arms back from around Adam's back to rub the itch away. As she did, she heard a faint knocking in the distance.

Olive ignored the sound, determined to enjoy the moment with her husband. However, the knocking sound rapped at Olive's subconscious, scratching at her nerves like an annoying thought in the back of her mind.

"I think someone is at the front door." She blurted.

"Just leave it be," Adam told her. "It's probably just a deer outside. You wouldn't hear someone knocking at the front of the house all the way back here."

The knocking sounded again, this time carrying from the front hall, past the staircase and dining room, skittering through the sitting room and continuing down the hallway and through the open kitchen door.

It bellowed into the space where Olive and Adam sat, making its presence undeniable.

Adam gasped. Olive gritted her teeth and stared through the kitchen door.

"That's it! I'm so sorry." She moved Adam aside and hopped down from the countertop onto the floor. "I'm going to be much calmer if I take care of this."

The knocking continued to reverberate through the house as Olive stomped back down the hallway, through the sitting room and dining room and into the front hall. Unlocking the large wooden front door, she forced it open with a scowl.

The person on the other side of the door was a seamstress from the palace. Her name was Rose, and she had worked very closely with Olive in the preceding weeks to sew and embroider the royal wedding dress. Rose was a young, smallish girl, presumably in her late teens. She had white-blonde hair and pale skin that lacked even a reddish tinge.

Rose shrunk back at the site of the angry princess. "I—I'm sorry, Miss. I mean, Princess. Am I disturbing you?"

Olive huffed, blowing a curl away from her face. "What is it, Rose?"

"I am sorry, Princess Olive. I just—I want to bring you this."

Rose held out a flat oval-shaped object for Olive. Olive sighed and took the gift, just as she felt Adam walk up behind her. The object was a mounted piece of embroidery work in the style of a wall plaque. Across a light blue background were understated silver and gold stars coupled with light green and white wispy clouds, and wisps representing a light breeze. The words *Love thy neighbor* floated across the background of the plaque in bubbly cloud-like lettering.

Olive was annoyed. The plaque she held was nothing special. Rose could have waited until the next day before delivering it.

"Oh, look, Adam. It's blue," Olive cooed with sarcasm.

"Blue?" Adam mimicked her tone. "What do you know? Blue seems to be the color of the day!"

"Blue has been today's color, hasn't it?" Olive agreed. "You know what else is blue, dear?"

"My manhood, if we don't get some privacy," Adam sneered. "You know, Rose, my wife and I were just finishing up our discussion on the color blue when we heard a knock at the door. And look… more blue! Surely we don't have enough blue already!"

Olive pursed her lips and looked at the plaque. "Rose, dear, it says 'love thy neighbor', but as you can see, we have no neighbors here at all. We are up here on this hill high above the rest of Sidney. We're a quarter mile from the palace walls, and nearly half a mile from any of the other houses. *Why* would you give this to us, and why… Just *why* would you knock on our door for so long? All we've been wanting is some privacy and some peace, and it's just not happening. I wish you would have just come back another day!"

Rose lowered her chin another inch. "I'm sorry, Princess. It's just that—I thought you said you liked blue. I even traded me favorite kerchief for a blue one so I could use it in the background for you. And the reason I knocked so many times is because I walked all the way here on me own and didn't want to have to make the trip again tomorrow. I'm sorry, Miss—Princess. Princess Olive—I'm so sorry!"

"Okay, well, uh, next time you want to walk over here, maybe don't do it when it's starting to get dark like this, because now you know you'll have to walk back too. It can be dangerous," Olive lectured. "Please leave us alone now. Go. Away!"

And with that, Olive slammed the door in Rose's face.

"Stupid girl," Adam snapped. "Take a hint!"

"I like Rose, Adam," Olive told him. "She and I have become quite close over the last few weeks, and I do consider her a friend. I'm just—so annoyed with her right now, and with everyone else, too! I'll patch things up with her later. I mean, it's not like she can sabotage my dress anymore."

CHAPTER 2
Rose the Strange
*The Palace Gardens; One Month Before the Royal
Wedding*

Olive was impatient as she sat in the palace gardens. The garden was beautiful and peaceful, and had she had a book and a cup of tea, she could have allowed herself to enjoy it. She wasn't there to soak up the serenity, though. Instead, she was waiting to be presented with embroidery samples, which she would use to choose her seamstress.

The concept seemed trivial and irrelevant to Olive. She would have thought the cut and fit of the dress would be more telling of a seamstress's abilities than the design that would lay atop the final product. Olive had a whole mess of ideas on how to improve productivity inside the palace. On her first day planning the royal wedding, she'd joined the bakers in the palace kitchen to show them how to mix a proper cake batter. After that, however, she was instructed to trust the royal process and not to interject. She obliged, but only because it was easier than arguing.

"Mi—Miss Princess." The first seamstress, Rose, stammered as she entered the garden. She approached the ornate bench where Olive sat but kept her gaze down at her own feet. "I want to show you me stitching sample. I do hope you like it."

Olive examined the embroidery hoop Rose handed her. The design inside the circle danced with subtle silver and gold stars backed by wisps of light green and deep blue against white lace fabric. The pattern was like the night sky, but also bright and awake, like daytime. It was simple enough to allow the white of the dress to stay prominent, yet intricate enough that one could not help but study its patterns up close.

"This is beautiful, Rose!" Olive told her. "And just my style."

"So you like it?" Rose exclaimed.

"I truly do. I'm willing to make my decision right now, already, and have you join me for a cup of tea with me here in the garden. I just have one question for you."

"Erm, of course, Princess? And I would love to join you for tea. But, what is your question?'

"Can you sew? Not just make pretty designs like this, but really sew?" Olive started. "Can you make me something that will fit well and still be comfortable, but that won't make me look boxy?"

Rose looked confused by the question, as if she was surprised Olive had even asked it. "Well, of course, Miss. I sew all me own clothes because I never has anyone else to do it for me. I always has. Don't have no other option."

Rose stepped back and fanned the skirt of her dress, turning to show Olive her plain brown and tan dress. She blushed as she did. "It's not nearly as fancy as I'm sure you might be used to, I'm afraid. But I don't like looking boxy myself, so I won't never sew anyone else up that way."

Olive smiled and nodded. "I'm not quite as fancy as you'd expect, Rose, but thank you. I grew up wearing dresses very similar to what you're wearing now. Most of mine were blue, though."

Rose's face lit up. "Blue? Oh, I dream of owning enough blue cloth for a dress. Did you sew them yourself, Princess?"

"No." Olive shook her head. "My brother did, for the most part. I did most of the cooking chores instead. I don't know much about sewing, which I know is strange for a girl."

Rose shook her head back. "Please don't call yourself strange, Miss. It's not kind."

Olive wrinkled her nose and chuckled. "No, Rose. I am a bit strange, and I'm not ashamed of it. I don't want to be like everyone else."

Rose looked down at her feet, slouching her shoulders and frowning. "They call me strange every day, Princess. I don't like it."

"Who calls you that?"

Rose's shoulders hunched lower. She shook her head but refused to look back up at Olive.

"Rose." Olive handed the embroidery sample back. "I would like you to sew my wedding dress, and embroider it with this pattern. I also would enjoy it if you'd stay for a cup of tea. However, I would like you to please tell me what's on your mind? You seem upset, and I think you want to tell me why."

Rose sighed and glanced at Olive before focusing her attention on the detail inside the embroidery loop, her mood more somber than before. "Thank you for the job, Miss. I am honored to work with you."

"Just honored?" Olive asked. "Rose, you seemed so excited just a few moments ago. Is there anything more you'd like to tell me? Who is it that's been cruel to you?"

Rose sighed. "Sometimes I wish the world was much different, Princess. I wish we could all have a chance to be great no matters how strange or poor we are. I wish that it didn't matter what family you was born to, that anyone could be royalty if you just work really hard to get there. I wish I could be important and famous and have queens and princesses from all over begging to have me sew dresses just for them."

Olive thought before responding. "Well, Rose, things like that are certainly possible. It's happened before, right here in Sidney."

"With you, Princess?"

"No." Olive chuckled. "With my grandfather. He opened his first butcher shop over sixty years ago. It was just a tiny store on the far side of Sidney, but people just loved visiting his shop. A few years later, he opened a bakery next door, and then a large restaurant near the commons. My father took over for him several years later, and he and my mother opened another restaurant on the mainland and then a bigger, fancier bakery near the Sidney commons! People from all over come to Sidney to eat at Grimm's."

Rose cleared her throat. "That's a fine story, Princess, but I want the chance not only to be a palace seamstress in Sidney, but for palaces on the mainland and across seas and all over! I want to be able to take boats to far-away lands where I can work with different types of cloth, silk or velvet maybe, and all different people, too. I saw pictures in a book about India once! I want to work with dresses like that one day."

Olive paused for several moments before responding. "Well, Rose. I'm sure if you put your mind to it, you may find a way to do all that one day. I hope you do. Now—are you able to tell me who it is who's been making fun of you?"

Rose glanced at Olive for a split second before staring at her feet once again. "Well, one of the young men in the palace who says cruel things to me is, well—it's your fiancé, Miss. Prince Adam calls me those names."

CHAPTER 3
The Super Moon
The Day After the Royal Wedding

Adam and Olive stumbled up to their bedroom early, tired and cranky from their frustrating day.

The romantic mood from earlier was gone, and Olive craved some quiet time before settling down to sleep. She lit an oil lamp and brought it into her dressing room to be alone for the first time in what seemed like weeks. The dressing room was a large closet attached to her and Adam's bedroom, lit by only a few small, stained-glass windows near the very top of the east-side walls. Adam had designed the room to allow the princess privacy, but also to let in enough light while she dressed in the mornings.

She sat cross-legged on the floor in front of a large oval mirror near the back of the room, which she knew was very un-princess-like, but she didn't care. Setting the lamp on the floor beside her, she parted and twisted locks of her long, dark hair into four fat curls, two on each side of her head. It had been her hair-setting routine for as long as she could remember.

Adam was sitting in a large bay window in their bedroom with a sketchbook when Olive returned. She'd changed into a silk nightgown she'd found among the many gorgeous clothes and accessories Adam had stocked in the dressing room for her.

He looked up at her with a calm smile. "I like your hair that way."

"Thank you, but it's not a hairstyle. I'm only wearing it this way so it curls."

"Well, I think you should wear it like that for real one day and see how many compliments you get. It's cute on you."

"You are quite silly sometimes, Adam." She joined him at the open bay window. "What are you drawing? Isn't it too dark soon to draw anything you see out there?"

"The moon is bright and very full tonight. It wants to inspire me, but I'm not sure what it's telling me yet."

Olive loved watching her husband use his creative talents. She gave him a kiss on the cheek and crawled into bed, facing the window until the light grew darker and the cool air rolled in, lulling her to sleep.

Olive's eyes opened to see the light of morning. She felt as though she'd only slept a short time, however, and Adam hadn't moved from his seat at the window.

"Why are you still awake, dear?" she asked.

Adam gestured for her to join him. "Come closer, Olive! Look with me."

Olive was sleepy. She didn't want to leave the comfort of the warm bed, but Adam seemed adamant for her to join him. She pulled herself up to sit with him on the window seat, expecting to view a typical morning sky. The scene they looked out onto didn't appear to be morning at all, however. Olive rubbed her eyes and yawned before straining to get a better look.

"It's strange, isn't it?" Adam asked.

The sky above them was a medium hue of blue scattered with a million colorful stars that blinked and twinkled in every shade of white, gold, green, and blue, some of them even changing colors as they blinked. The moon was the oddest looking of all, appearing bright orange and several times larger than any other night.

In comparison, the ground below was calm and much darker than the sky above it. The garden was dim and hard to see from their place at the window, which was similar to any ordinary night. It seemed that only the sky above them was active and bright, as if it was a second layer of atmosphere hosting a wild party while the bottom layer remained sleepy and calm.

Olive peered down at Adam's sketchbook, not surprised to see that he'd been working on a drawing of the scene outside.

He winked up at her from his sitting position. "I call it the supermoon."

Olive said nothing, but a lump formed in her throat as she examined the drawing. She felt both intrigued and uneasy as she tried to make sense of it.

"What? You don't like supermoon? Do you prefer crazy-moon? Wild-moon?" Adam made a short howling sound, like a wolf.

"What you've drawn here—" Olive started. "It's just like the embroidery design from my wedding dress."

Adam stopped sketching. His lips twisted, and he held out the sketchbook in front of him. "I suppose it's similar, but your dress didn't have a moon shape on it, did it? Just stars and wispy bits."

She paused for a long moment. "Perhaps you're right. I am quite tired, so I'm likely just confused." Olive kissed his forehead and sauntered back towards the bed.

Adam was right. Her wedding dress lacked the shape of a moon in the embroidery. Yet, in so many other ways, his drawing mimicked the pattern found on both her dress as well as the plaque Rose had brought for them. The sense of unease, Olive realized, was at least in-part from the guilt she felt about the way she and Adam had turned Rose away.

Olive tried to shake the feeling away without success. She knew the thoughts were better left for the morning, and that any negative emotion mixed with exhaustion only made things worse, but this made it harder to ignore her guilt. She was also a bit scared — not of anything in particular, but rather, of the impending doom chilling her body, dragging her into a broken slumber.

CHAPTER 4
Dust, Hair and Cobwebs
Day Two

Several hours later, a scratching sound woke Olive from her shallow rest. The window shutters were closed now, and it was too dark to see around the room.

Her ears began itching as she turned over and heard the scratching sound again. It was a soft noise, one she might have brushed off as a subconscious chittering if she had been more relaxed.

"I swear, if we have mice already, Adam," Olive whispered under her breath as she pulled back the covers. Her feet were bare, and as she climbed out of bed, she noticed the wooden floorboards underneath the bed felt dusty.

The walls and floor also creaked around her as she stood, which was an odd thing to happen in such a new home. She stood and scurried across the cold, rough floor of the bedroom towards the door to the hallway where she had heard the scuffling sound. Olive touched the doorknob to discover that it was colder than she'd expected. She opened the door, and the doorknob stuck to her hand for a moment as she tried letting go. It was icy, she realized.

Olive couldn't see anything at all through the darkness in the hallway, but the scratching noise had finally ceased, so she turned to head back into the bedroom. A small breeze passed through the house just then, kicking up dust from the floor and blowing it into Olive's eyes.

"Ouch!" she shouted aloud. The dust stung, and the burning only worsened as she tried to wipe it away. She stumbled backwards towards the bed, but had barely made it across the threshold of the bedroom door when the breeze from the hallway returned. The breeze grew stronger and colder until heavy gusts of wind whipped around Olive, throwing off her balance. With the wind came debris, leaves, sticks, and other sharp pieces of earth that pummeled her skin and hair.

"Adaaam!" she called, but even her own voice sounded as if it was miles away, and Adam didn't respond.

The air became wet and very cold. Olive couldn't see anything or sense any of her surroundings aside from the painful, discombobulating winds. With some struggle, she crouched close to the ground and pulled her knees to her chest, wrapping her arms around them for warmth and durability. A moment later, she felt the floorboards as she dropped into a kneel.

Her eyes were still burning, and the winds still circled around her, but she thought she heard Adam's voice just then: very soft and far, far away.

"Olive!" He was closer now. "Olive! Are you okay, dear?!"

"I'm right here, Adam! Can you hear me?" she called. She listened for Adam's voice as the breeze and flurry of debris dissipated. Her eyes stopped burning, and the floorboards softened. A gentle, fluffy sensation hugged her waist and legs. She was able to open them to see the bright light of morning and Adam's worried face above her. She was safe in bed, the air around her calm and still.

"Oh, my!" Olive breathed a loud sigh of relief, though her heart was still beating hard and fast. "I was stuck in a storm, but now I'm—"

"You had a nightmare," Adam snickered as he kissed her forehead. "Welcome back to reality, Princess."

She rolled her eyes and then reached upwards to kiss him. His chin and upper lip were scruffy, as if he hadn't shaved in days.

"You're like a wolf," she sputtered. "When was the last time you shaved?"

"Your hair isn't too pretty, either, right now," he teased.

"I told you, this is just to set it," she said. "Anyway, I thought you liked it this way."

Adam's eyes widened. "Let's just say I can see now why you don't wear it like that."

"You are so mean," Olive teased back. "Go to the palace and have a servant teach you how to shave."

"What the hell, Olive? Why can you say I look like a wolf, but I can't tell you that your hair looks ridiculous?"

"I'm sorry, Adam, that was rude of me. I didn't sleep well, and that nightmare put me in a bad place. I'm going to get up and get dressed so I can take a walk and clear my head." She threw off the covers and turned towards the dressing room. The floor creaked, and soon as she could feel the cold, dirty debris underneath her feet again.

"Fuck," Olive snapped, stunned. For the first time since she'd woken, she looked around the bedroom, her heart sinking.

"What is it?" Adam responded. He was still under the covers but sat up straight to join her.

She looked back at him, at his furry face and scraggly hair, then back at the rest of the room, then down at the floor, where her bare feet felt dry and scaly against the rough wood.

Adam had designed the room to be a sanctuary for the young couple, blending regality with comfort and modern style. The large bay window, adorned with maroon and gold cushioning, had been the focal point of the room. Surrounding the window was an indulgence of creature comforts: a chaise lounge with a velvet throw, two tall shelves filled with books and art supplies, an easel, a small harp Olive had been excited to learn to play, and a mirrored vanity stocked with an assortment of perfumes, jewelry, combs, barrettes and more. The solid wooden floors had been shiny and smooth, stained a dark mahogany to compliment the rest of the decor.

Everything in the room had been polished and new the day of the royal wedding, every stitch intact and every earring in its place. Adam had made sure of it before allowing Olive to see it for the first time. And yet now, as Olive stared at a dusty cobweb in the corner of the ceiling, none of that even seemed possible.

The floors were no longer dark and shiny. Rather, the wood was rough, faded, and splintered. Every surface of the room was covered with dirt and dust. Even the curtains were withered and full of holes.

Adam's expression was blank; he said nothing. If there was movement on his face at all, it was in his beard, which seemed to be growing thicker by the minute. He sat motionless for a long time, staring towards the window where he'd been drawing just a few hours earlier. His mouth was half-open like he was about to say something, though he continued to stay silent.

Olive followed his gaze towards the window. The decorative cushioning was gone, leaving only the bare, splintered wood of the seat and a thick layer of dust that crept up around the faded curtains. Dirty cobwebs hung from the corners of the walls. Even the metal on the bedposts was tarnished and worn.

The two sat speechless. It was as if the room had aged a hundred years overnight.

"Adam?" Olive spoke after several minutes. She sat next to him on the bed, rubbing his shoulder in an aimless attempt to comfort him.

He groaned at the contact, and she retracted her arm. The painful silence in the air coupled with their utter confusion had caused a raucous stampede of questions inside Olive's head that forced her off the bed. She paced the room, tense.

"Where are you going?" Adam asked.

She paused, fidgeting, "I don't know, Adam. I just can't sit much longer. There has to be an explanation for what's happened."

Adam scoffed. "What are you talking about? None of this is possible!"

"It's real, Adam, and it's happening now! I believe it's best to try and find someone who may know more?"

He didn't make eye contact with her. He only sighed and stared into a corner of the room, frowning. He used one of his large, hairy hands to wipe tears from his cheeks.

"Why is the hair on your arms so thick this morning?" she asked him. "Does it often grow like that?"

He didn't answer, but a low, deep sound rumbled from deep within his diaphragm.

"Are you ill, dear?" she asked, approaching him with an extended arm.

"Don't touch me!" Adam shouted, turning back towards her and swatting her hand away. "And don't look at me like that. You look terrible, too!"

The walls trembled around them as he shouted, causing Olive to back away in fear. As she did, something sharp pricked her bare foot. She gasped, lifting her foot to see a piece of glass sticking out from it, and a broken hand mirror on the floor below. In the shards, she caught a glimpse of herself. Even through her fractured reflection, she could see that, like everything else in the bedroom, she too did not look like herself.

Her dark hair had always been thick and unruly, but she had always paid special attention to setting and styling it. She'd made a habit of pulling it back and covering it with a thin scarf at the bakery, and she took the time each morning and night to comb out any dirt or tangles. She had often been praised for her beautiful hair, many agreeing that it was her best physical quality. Now, however, even though only a sliver of hair and face around her temple were visible in the broken mirror, something was different. Her face and hair were unhealthy and wrong.

She approached the vanity and used her hand to wipe away the thick dust from the mirror, realizing that Adam had not been wrong about how terrible she looked. Even on her worst days, she never imagined she could look like the woman who stared back at her now. Her face was sallow and pale, her brown eyes sunken and lined with purplish veins. Her lips were so white and chapped that they disappeared into her colorless skin. She used a dirty finger to rub the blueish-grey circle underneath one of her eyes, as it looked at first glance to be blotted with soot. The area felt sore and raw, though, and the darkness did not wipe clear. She frowned and whimpered, wincing as she wiped the dust from a larger area on the mirror. A patch of clumped, knotted hair came into view against her temple.

As she searched the vanity for a comb, she realized that the neatly organized items which had been laid out on the vanity just the night before were no longer nice and no longer organized. Dust and grime covered the combs, brushes, and powder tins. She gagged as she pushed aside a small, cracked plate with a stale crust of pastry near the mirror. The items were not only dirty, she realized, but also appeared to have endured heavy use.

Regardless, Olive located a grimy, wide-toothed comb and took it to the mass of hair against her temple.

"What are you doing?" Adam's voice boomed from where he still sat on the bed behind her.

She paused and let out a hopeless sigh. "Trying to get this tangle out."

He chuckled, though he sounded angry. "*That's* what you're concerned about right now? Your hair? Have you looked around?"

She turned back to him. "Well, you don't seem too interested in doing anything about it! Shall we go find help together?"

Adam stared at her for a moment and then looked down at his lap. He said nothing.

"I didn't think you'd want to go," Olive said, half snide and half disappointed. "I'll be in my dressing room."

She slammed the door and locked it behind her, feeling so irritated, she could swear her ears were almost hissing. The dressing room was dim, with only a small stained-glass window above letting in a cloud of pink light from inside. She could see an assortment of thinning, dusty dresses on hangers against the far wall. A thick smell, like musty fabric, hung in the air and irritated her eyes. She used her fingers to try and rub the feeling away, but it only caused her eyes to burn and itch again.

"Olive!" Adam grumbled from outside the door.

"Please let me be!" Her voice was harsher than she'd intended.

"Let me in!" Adam banged his fist against the door.

She gritted her teeth and ignored him, turning to look at herself in the full-length mirror, which was now distressed and cracked in several places. Her heart sank as her disheveled reflection stared back at her. Just like everything else, the four fat curls she'd twisted the night before had changed; her pale and sunken face was now framed by four snakelike chunks of tangled, matted hair, two on each side of her head.

CHAPTER 5
Stale with Mold & Grime

"It's like there was a storm, and we just slept through it," Adam mused.

Olive had returned to the bedroom, but now stood near the door to the hallway, her arms crossed over her chest. Adam was still on the bed, sitting cross-legged with his hands cupped around his face.

"My nightmare was about a storm," she offered, shrugging.

"Maybe it wasn't a dream, then." Adam suggested. "Or maybe we're dreaming now?"

She huffed and rolled her eyes, irritability consuming her.

"Why aren't you listening to me!" Adam whined.

Frustrated, Olive tried to run her fingers through her hair, realizing it wasn't possible in its current condition. "We have to go to the palace," she told him. "We need to go talk with someone."

"No!" he shouted at her. "They'll send someone, I'm sure of it. Someone must be on their way right now. We should stay."

"I'm leaving to find help," she decided. "You can either join me or stay here, but I can't just sit here expecting someone to come and rescue us."

"Please stay with me!" he whined again. "They can't just leave us here like this. They've sent someone to help already, I know they have."

"Adam," she began, "if you would like to sit here and wait, then that is your choice, but that's not the way I do things. I'm heading to the palace with or without you."

"Do you know what your problem is, Olive? You're too impatient! I'm sure this is all just because of the moon last night. Perhaps it caused that storm you dreamt about? The palace will send people to look for us."

She gaped at him. "Are you listening to yourself? Didn't you *just* say you thought none of this is possible? I said I wanted to go find a logical explanation, and now you're saying that help is on the way? Did the palace raise you to do absolutely nothing for yourself?"

Adam opened his mouth to answer, but said nothing, although he was frowning.

Olive softened as she saw the damaged look on her husband's face. She spoke again, but quieter, and with more patience. "Adam—as a Grimm, I was always taught to take care of myself, so that's what I'm going to do. You can stay here if you like, or you can come along with me, but I can't let myself stay here and blindly wait for help."

Olive spotted Adam's riding boots near the bedroom door and began to pull them on over her slippers.

"Why are you wearing my boots?" Adam asked.

"Because the shoes in my closet are too dainty and uncomfortable for trekking across town." She gave him an awkward smile. "You sure you don't want to go?"

Adam shook his head and frowned.

Olive gave a quick, firm nod before venturing out of the bedroom into the creaky, dirty hallway. The house was dark, and the air around her smelled of mold and grime. She crept down the staircase, making sure to avoid several broken stairs and numerous areas of splintered wood along the way. Step by step, she made her way to the front foyer, where the dulled marble floors were littered with glass, dirt, and dried leaves from a dozen shattered vases and flower-pots. It occurred to her that she was standing in the exact spot where she and Adam had been intimate just the day before.

As Olive turned the tarnished door handles and pulled open the large double doors, her hands were shaking a lot faster than she'd noticed. She was nervous and scared, she realized, expecting to find a storm-trodden scene with broken branches and eerie winds on the other side.

The first thing she noticed was the happy chatter of birds and the sun against her face. The air was still and calm and crisp, and dried autumn leaves rustled about in the front gardens. There was no sign that a storm had been through.

The front gardens, however, were unkempt and in disarray. The grass was tall and browning. Spindles of dark brush and wilted vines lived where rose bushes had been. On the day of the royal wedding, the grounds around the home had been groomed to perfection. Now, grapevines and other shrubberies shrouded in dewy spiderwebs and rotting leaves bordered the property. A sparse wooded forest beyond that restricted her view of the town below.

Olive trudged across the garden, pulling aside bits and pieces of brush to clear a view of the town. Though she was nearly a quarter mile above it, she could see that Sidney looked the same as she'd always known it.

Olive let out a heavy sigh of relief. A cold breeze blew underneath her nightdress as she did. She looked down at herself, realizing that in her haste to leave the house, she'd neglected getting dressed.

The air felt much colder once she started down the shaded path to the palace, and the nightdress now seemed as much an irresponsible choice as a silly one. Crickets chirped around her; a pair of chipmunks danced and squeaked around her feet.

"Move along. Please don't nip me." She swatted at the happy rodents below, who answered back in mocking tones before bounding forward, squeakeling in sing-song unison. Olive watched as the tiny animals slipped with ease through a wall of metallic rings on the path ahead.

The pink stone wall that had surrounded the palace was gone. In its place, there stood a tall, sturdy metal grate with circular gaps that allowed her to see through to the other side. On the other side stood an impressive white house with a wrap-around porch and a sprawling green lawn stamped with colorful flower patches and ornate shrubberies. The gardens were open and bright, encircling the house and leading up the place where Olive stood, slumped and stumped, at the edge of the woods.

She itched with bewilderment, yearning for an explanation. She thought of the times in her childhood when she or her siblings had thrown temper tantrums whenever they were confused, and how the behavior had grown less and less appropriate as she aged. Now, however, faced with the unfamiliar environment and a rapid stream of unanswered questions, a lump formed in her throat and tears welled in her eyes. Sniffling, Olive sank to her knees and wailed, a puddle of flailing limbs and tears on the damp ground.

Curling into the fetal position, staring without emotion at the dull sheen of the metal grate next to her, she whined, "The castle—the king and queen—what's happened to Sidney?!"

"Well, hello there!" came a man's voice from behind her.

Startled, she sat up to face the direction of the voice, brushing a clump of mud from her cheek. The man was large in every way: tall, with broad shoulders and a strong, muscular build. He was well-dressed and grinned widely, showing-off a set of shiny white teeth.

"Who are you? Where is the palace? Where is the king?" Olive demanded. She eyed him with caution as she wiped mud and tears from her face.

The man looked Olive up and down. He blinked several times and shook his head, "I can't say I understand your question, Miss. Although, if you're wanting to speak to the head counselor, I don't think he'll take you seriously looking like that. I suggest you find a place to wash up first. Maybe put some fresh clothing on and comb your hair out a bit."

Olive sniffled and wiped her nose on her sleeve. "I, um—I can't do those things right now."

"Suit yourself—literally," he scoffed. "I'd love to help, but, 'Can't?' Now there's a word. I won't help you if you refuse to help yourself." He shrugged and turned back in the direction from which he'd come.

"No. Wait! Please don't leave! Where is the king? What is a head counselor? Are you able to get me into the palace to see him?"

The man turned back to Olive, raising a befuddled eyebrow. "Get some help, lady. This is beyond what I can offer you."

Olive's temper boiled again in an instant. She stood and began jumping up and down and then lurching towards the man. "No! You don't understand! I'm a princess! Listen to me! Listen to me! Listen to me! There was a castle here yesterday. Right there! Not just a castle—a whole palace! There was a storm. It's all different now. I need your help! Please don't leave me! I'm just—so confused!"

But the man had already turned his back and was walking away. He didn't turn around again.

CHAPTER 6
Ragged & Restless

Olive had always been good at keeping composed when the situation called for it. On the rare occasion where she let herself cause a scene, it was strategic or to make a point. The way she'd acted around the man, however, was out of true despair.

After a moment, though, something changed. She stopped crying and stood upright, as if pulled upwards by something in the sky. She walked towards the town commons with newfound energy, wearing a courageous grin and feeling quite confident.

Near the edge of the town commons walked a young mother with two small children: a boy and a girl. The children danced and sang with each other around the woman's legs. The boy began spinning out of control, his shoulder knocking into one of Olive's knees.

"I'm sorry about him, ma'am," the woman apologized.

"Your child does not own the common grounds!" Olive snapped at the woman, surprised by her own curtness. "Get control of him!"

The woman looked Olive up and down and curled her lip in disgust before gathering and leading the children in the opposite direction.

"What? That's it? You're just going to walk away without apologizing?" The words fell out of Olive's mouth for reasons she couldn't understand, followed by feelings to match. Her face turned red with anger; searing pain shot through her temples, and her ears hissed.

The woman shot Olive a second dirty look, but this time the women's glares locked. All sound drained away except for the hissing inside Olive's ears.

The young mother's glare softened; her eyes dulled, and her face drooped as her jaw went slack. Olive could feel herself peering past the woman's face with each quickening breath. She could see behind her expression and into her soul, exploring her deepest worries and darkest insecurities. She relished in the woman's suppressed pain and misfortune, feeling everything the woman could feel, but without remorse or sympathy.

After several more seconds of powerful silence, Olive spoke.

"Do you really think anyone believes these two children are twins?" she asked the woman in an oily tone.

The young mother's eyes widened, and her lips twitched back into place. She looked bewildered, gathering the children to her side again. She appeared confused and flustered, but not afraid.

"Are you sick, Mummy?" one of the children asked.

The woman looked perturbed, but not as much as Olive would have expected given the invasive staring session. Olive wondered if the woman had even been aware of it at all. The woman's obliviousness confused Olive, fueling her fury even more.

"Excuse me! I am *talking* to you!" Olive shouted.

The woman placed a protective hand on her children's shoulders. "Mind your own business, you old hag!"

"You're not fooling anyone, sweetheart." Olive ignored her, her tone sinister but relaxed. "Of course, you remember the day you both went into labor? You first, and then your sister. Your poor whore of a little sister from the brothel. The one your disgusting husband always favored."

Olive knelt down so that the children could make eye contact with her, her voice coarse as she spoke. "David and Isabelle. Brother and sister, and also—cousins? Remember that, children. Remember this next time someone asks you about your twin sibling."

The mother and her children stood shocked and silent. The woman's eyes held tears until she spoke a moment later. "How could you know something like that? Why would you approach us like this?"

The hissing subsided and Olive felt drained, relieved—and overcome with regret and remorse.

"I, um—I don't know, exactly." Olive stammered. "I'm—I'm so sorry. It's been a very strange morning. Something went wrong, with Sidney, and— well, with me too, I think."

"You think?" The woman scoffed. "Stay away from my family, you ragged old woman, you—you witch!"

The woman pulled her children through the commons and away from Olive, leaving her standing there, overwhelmed with guilt and confusion. An intense wave of nausea and dizziness washed over her. She struggled to catch her breath, feeling as if she was spinning and falling into the Earth.

"Aw, don't faint on me now!" called a man's voice from nearby.

Olive turned towards the voice to see the large, handsome man she had met earlier holding his hand out to her. Her vision was shaky, and she realized that at some point she must have fallen because she was sitting on the ground in the center of the commons. She gathered herself up and brushed the dirt from her nightdress, accepting the man's hand.

"Olive Grimm," she said, shaking the man's hand firmly.

"Jepson," the man told her. "I own JB's Tavern over on the other side of Sidney. If you'd like, I can walk you over there and get you a drink. You look like you might need it."

Olive felt the need to isolate herself and regain composure before meeting anyone new. She was also uncomfortable with the idea that Jepson might be making a pass at her, albeit it unlikely in her current physical state. Still, the idea of a cold ale sounded wonderful and well-deserved. Rationalizing that mingling with the townspeople was the logical next step in the day's illogical events thus far, she decided to ask Adam to join her for a drink at the tavern.

"Let me just run home and change," she told him. "I'll meet you there in just a little bit."

"I'm gonna hold you to it. Here, take this with you." Jepson winked, tossing her a small, wrapped package. He then turned on his heel and strode off, humming a tune Olive didn't recognize.

Olive took the package under her arm and strolled back towards the decrepit house that was now her home. Once she arrived in the front garden, she settled on a tree stump and opened the package. Inside was a brick of chocolate. Olive was hungry; she had not eaten all day, and though chocolate sounded like a satisfying snack, she also realized the need to be cautious. Jepson was a stranger who had no apparent reason to be so generous.

She broke off a small chunk of the chocolate and tasted it. It was smooth and delicious, and her stomach groaned with approval, but she decided to set it aside for a while. She knew from working at the restaurant that if she didn't fall ill in a day's time, the chocolate had not yet spoiled, nor been intentionally tainted.

Adam had always had a weakness for sweets. It was, after all, how he and Olive had met and fallen in love. Knowing all too well that Adam wouldn't be as cautious or rational about the chocolate as she was, Olive wrapped it back in the brown paper and hid it on the ledge of a high windowsill outside of their home before heading inside to change.

CHAPTER 7
Dry & Salty

"Adam, dear! Hello!" Olive called to him as she walked into the house, but Adam didn't answer.

"Adam! The town is safe. I've—we've been invited out for a drink by one of the townspeople."

Again, there was no response. Worried, she headed up to their bedroom to look for him, without success. She yelled for him through the upstairs hall and then scampered back towards the stairs. She ran a bit too fast, though, twisting her ankle on a broken stair.

"Dammit! Adam, where are you?" She stood, her head spinning and her ankle throbbing in pain.

Steadying herself, she headed back to her dressing room to change her clothes. She forced a small smile while getting dressed, attempting to convince herself that the situation was under control. Her faux optimism stayed with her as she changed from the nightdress and boots into a musty and tattered yellow velvet dress and a beat-up pair of matching yellow slippers. Peering at herself in the broken mirror, she tried to see the matted locks around her head as the curls they once were. For just a moment, Olive believed she looked lovely.

Once again downstairs, she decided to check the back wings of the house for Adam before heading back into town. The optimistic feeling fell flat, though, as she reached the drawing room door. She knew that on the other side, the gorgeous and extravagant room Adam had spent so much time and creative energy designing would look as dreadful as the rest of the house.

She stepped inside, met with a strong odor of mildew and dust. The furniture was old, dirty, and torn. Even the art supplies on the shelves looked as if they had been used and reused. Out of the dozen stained glass windows bordering the upper walls of the room, only three were intact. The others had shattered, leaving the room open to the elements. Dead leaves, dirt, and sharp, colorful shards of stained glass littered the floor and furniture.

Adam was there, lying on the floor and facing the ceiling next to the chaise lounge. His eyes were gray and still, and his face was now sheathed in long, coarse hair. The hair on his head had also grown quite long since Olive had seen him earlier in the day.

"Adam?" Olive's voice cracked, barely above a whisper.

His chest moved up and down, but he said nothing.

"Adam, please talk to me."

He blinked a few times, and a look of despair came over his otherwise still face.

"What's happening to us, Olive?" he asked in a quiet, worried tone.

"I don't know. The world out there… It's different. Not bad, though. Do you want to go into town with me? You can shave and get dressed, and then we can have a look together."

"Dammit, Olive! You can't be serious!" Adam sat up with an energy that shook the room around them. A piece of stained glass hit the floor from a shelf high above.

She wracked her mind for a shred of positivity she could share with him in that moment. "I don't know what's serious and what isn't anymore," she started. "I know that whatever happened last night is strange and unusual and—physically impossible, but I don't think there's anything we can do right now besides continue to move forward until we figure out what we can do about it."

"Move forward?! How the hell are we supposed to move forward? We have no food, no clothes, no house, and no money! What are we going to do? What the hell are we going to do?"

"Adam, we *do* have a house, and we do have clothes. The rest—I don't know what's going to happen with that, but I do know that sitting here complaining about it isn't going to fix the problem."

"I'm not complaining!" The room shook again as he shouted from his supine position. Looking up at the broken stained-glass windows, silent tears rolled down his cheeks and onto his torn, yellowed shirt. For the first time, Olive noticed tufts of thick black hair poking out from between his shirt buttons.

"Have you tried shaving or cutting it?" she asked him.

He looked at her, tears continuing down his furry face. His breathing quickened, and a small, threatening, animal-like growl sounded from the back of his throat.

She stood with quiet caution and began backing away, but she couldn't look away from Adam's blackening eyes. "I'm going back into town to find some food," she said. "Would you like to go with me?"

His lips curled back around his teeth as he growled again, louder than before, "You did this!"

"I didn't do this, Adam. I couldn't have done this."

"We weren't supposed to move away from the palace! That was your idea. Things like this only happen when people move away from tradition. We're not supposed to do things like this!" His voice rose with each sentence he spoke.

"But, that doesn't even make sense, Adam! Where did you hear something like that?" Olive continued backing towards the hallway door, her fear growing with each step.

"It's common sense, Olive! You wouldn't know because you grew up as a peasant. You never wanted to be a princess, did you? You caused this! Your family—everyone knows the Grimms are wicked. My father told me your grandmother was burned in a witch hunt. The cookies—oh god. I should have known better. Why else would someone like me marry somebody like you?"

"What are you saying, Adam? That I cursed you? Do you know how mad that sounds? You're upset, I know, but please don't do this. Please, take a walk with me." She held her arms out to him but did not move closer.

"Don't touch me!" The room was shaking with fierce vigor now, and Adam howled at the ceiling.

One of the three remaining stained-glass windows shattered, and a large piece fell at his feet. He picked up the shard and shot it in the direction of Olive's upper body. She ducked to dodge it as the large piece of glass missed where her neck had been, shattering against the door behind her. She panicked. Her hands were trembling, but she was able to turn and open the drawing room door, swinging herself around into the hallway before slamming the door behind her.

Olive's whole body shook with fear as she sat against the door in the hallway. Adam didn't follow her, but instead continued to howl inside the drawing room, causing the door to vibrate against her back until the anger-induced energy in the house subsided again. Silence fell over the home just as the sun outside began to set. Olive no longer had any desire to meet Jepson at the tavern or to venture out into the town again. She hadn't even found a reason yet to move from her place against the drawing room door. She sat there for what seemed like hours, half-hoping the chocolate Jepson gave her had been poisoned. She imagined herself dying a slow and peaceful death right there in the hallway: an idea that was almost more tolerable than her current situation.

The thought of the chocolate reminded her she was still very hungry. Her thoughts shifted to mulling over a mental list of simple yet filling recipes she knew from memory, and she wondered which shelf-stable ingredients might still be stocked in the kitchen.

"Corn cakes," she whispered out loud.

The corn cakes she had in mind were not the most exciting meal, at least not without something to complement the dry flavor and texture. Her family had often made these particular corn cakes during winter months to place at the bottom of bowls of soup. The recipe, made from a simple mixture of cornmeal, salt, soda ash, and water, resulted in bland, brittle pancakes that would soak up the flavor of soups without becoming too soggy.

Her stomach groaned in approval, even at the thought of the boring meal. She smiled, wondering what her brothers would think if she told them how excited she felt to eat corn cakes, and it helped her to feel optimistic again. Olive stood, placing her hand against the drawing room door, knowing her husband lay miserable and dangerous on the other side. He was so quiet now, as if none of it had even happened.

"You must be hungry," she whispered against the door. Then she turned away and made for the kitchen.

She made sure to lock the door behind her before surveying the condition of the kitchen. The skylight windows were cracked and filthy; a few of them had shattered or were missing. A pile of dry leaves sat in the far corner underneath an empty pane. The pile crinkled as a slight breeze came through the open space above. The rest of the kitchen was grimy and contained a faint smell of molding bread. Several canisters remained intact in an area of the counter tiled with paintings of different stringed instruments.

Olive touched a counter tile with a painting of a mandolin. "Oh, Adam," she whispered. "You really do love me. You're just hungry and confused."

She shuddered again at the thought of Adam's behavior in the drawing room. She remembered his lips curling back, his growl, the blackening of his eyes, and the way he had used the shard of glass as a weapon against her.

She took a few deep breaths and steadied her thoughts. "I know you didn't mean it, dear."

She wiped away a handful of tears and shifted her focus back to cooking and feeling positive again, opening each of the dry ingredient canisters on the counter to see what could be salvaged. The wheat and barley flours, brown sugar, and oats had all spoiled. The cornmeal, salt, cinnamon, white flour, white sugar, soda ash, honey, and several herbs and spices had all held up much better than expected.

She gathered sticks and spring water near the creek outside their home and found a striker in a kitchen drawer to light the kindling reservoir underneath the stovetop. It was a lot of work, but Olive was able to make six perfect-looking corn cakes. She sprinkled each with a little cinnamon and sugar and drizzled them with honey. The cakes looked pretty sitting on the two plates, and Olive hoped Adam would be able to see past how dull and dry they would taste.

Tiptoeing out into the dining room with the two plates, she dusted off one side of the table and made it look as neat and clean as possible. She managed a small, very quiet knock on the drawing room door. "Adam, I've made us some food. Will you join me for dinner?"

She heard nothing, so she knocked again, this time louder. "Adam, dinner!"

Even though she had asked him to come out, Olive was startled as Adam opened the door. He stood in the doorway, looking defeated. He'd been crying but appeared calm.

"What did you make?" he asked.

"Pancakes," she told him. "They aren't great, but they'll do for now."

He managed a small smile and wrapped his arms around her. "You are amazing, my dear. I'm so sorry about earlier."

Olive said nothing as she hugged him back. She almost cried again but held it back, and she could feel in his hug that he was sorry.

"I called you wicked," he sobbed. "I said horrible things to my beautiful wife. I almost hurt you, too. If you hadn't ducked out of the way, I—"

"Adam," she interrupted him. "Honey, I'm sure you're starved. Let's go eat."

His eyes lit up when he saw the pancakes on the table. "Where did you get all this?" he asked.

"I made it from stuff you stocked in my kitchen."

"Olive, no!" he shouted. "We can't eat that stuff. It's old and probably spoiled! We're going to get sick!"

She stood her ground. "Well, we have to eat something. I've been baking my entire life, so I can tell when an ingredient has gone bad. The stuff I used to make this was still just fine."

"But how?" he whined. "How is that even possible? It's old. Everything is just—so *old!"* The room shook with his last word.

"Adam, dry ingredients are made to stay fresh indefinitely if stored well," she reasoned, fearing he'd become angry again if she didn't control the situation.

He lifted his furry face from where he'd rested it in his hairy hands to look at her. "Are you sure?"

"Yes," she sighed. "We used to use our less popular flours for years and years in my family's restaurants. Those canisters you chose—they preserved the ingredients perfectly. Thank you."

Olive was unsure if the logic was as sound as she was portraying it to be. Her priority wasn't as much the quality, or even the safety of the food anymore, as it was about keeping Adam calm.

Adam smiled at her. It was difficult to decipher with all his newfound facial hair, but she smiled back.

The two were only minutes into their corn cake dinner when Adam slammed his fork down on the table.

"What kind of pancakes are these? They taste weird. Bland, grainy, kind of salty. Just not great."

Olive pursed her lips, swallowed her frustration, and steadied herself. "We have limited resources. I know this isn't the food we're used to, but it's food, and we're both very hungry, so please just eat."

"It's just—you usually make such great food. I'm sure you can make something better than this."

Appalled, she tried to find a suitable response for him through her racing thoughts. She was enraged, though. Her temples throbbed with pain, and her ears began hissing again.

"Adam, we're in a dire situation right now. We have almost nothing to eat. There's a town out there, and

I'm sure I can get a job or something so we can eat better than this, but for now, this is all we have."

His face was angry now behind his whiskers. "Job? You want to get a job? Olive, you are the princess of Sidney! You don't work anymore!"

"I'm not a princess anymore, Adam. At least right now I'm not. I don't know why or how, but the palace is gone, and it doesn't sound like there's a king and queen anymore either. It's all different out there now. I tried to tell you. I wanted you to go with me to see for yourself. I'm sorry." Her fury subsided into sadness; the hissing in her ears stopped, as did the pain in her temples.

But the scowl on Adam's face hadn't changed. He picked up his plate of corn cakes and hurled it at the wall, howling at the ceiling again. He began pacing the front hall, causing the floor to shake with each of his steps.

"I'm so sorry I had to tell you this way," she cried.

He turned to her and huffed. "Why are you sorry? Why are you so calm? Are you—are you happy about all this? Do you think this is fun? We may never see our families again! Why are you not upset about that?"

"I am *not* settled with any of this! I don't know how to fix it, but if we just work on moving forward instead of—"

"Moving forward? Olive, why are we still talking about this? Do you think we'll just forget about the way things used to be? We'll just get peasant jobs and build this peasant house back up, and then we'll just be poor peasants and eat terrible peasant food! We are royalty, Olive. This is not how we're supposed to live."

The hissing whispered in her ears again.

"You, Prince Adam, are a spoiled brat!" she shouted. "I don't know what's going to happen to us! Maybe we'll find a way out of this, and things will go back to the way they were before, but maybe they won't! I don't know. What I do know is that we will never ever fix any of this by sitting around doing nothing and fighting with each other!"

Soon, the hissing was all she could hear again. Pain burrowed into her temples, aggravating every nerve in its path. She felt the same surge of strength and confidence she'd felt earlier in the town commons. As if by instinct, she stomped across the room to where Adam was pacing, getting in his way and glaring at him. The room stopped shaking, and Adam stopped pacing. His face went cold, and he stared back at her with blank, black eyes.

The feeling of fury grew until the hissing consumed her senses. She stared into Adam's pathetic blank expression, past his eyes and into his soul until she could see his woes and deepest insecurities. He'd felt sad and hopeless since he'd awoken that morning; he and Olive's home had been his largest personal accomplishment; giving him a grandiose feeling of satisfaction that had stayed with him each day since building it. Now that it was an entropic, decayed mess, he felt as if all his hard work had been for nothing. He wanted some time to feel sad and mourn the loss of the house, but Olive wanted him to help her find food or people who could help them, despite admitting she was capable of it herself. Olive was much too calm and sure of herself that the palace was gone. None of this made any sense, and none of it was fair for Adam. He was a prince; he shouldn't have to deal with this degree of chaos and disorder. And yet Olive was trying to force him to be a part of it. He'd decided he wouldn't have any of it. He'd remembered hearing a rumor that Olive's great aunt had been burned at the stake for witchcraft. He'd never asked Olive about it, but there had sometimes been talk around Sidney that her family still toyed with the dark arts. He'd never believed it in the past, but now Adam wondered if Olive had found a way to curse them into this situation. It was her fault, he'd concluded; there was no other explanation.

The pain and hissing quieted again, though Olive remained angry. She continued to stare into Adam's eyes, having no words to express her disappointment in what she had seen.

Adam's face changed from vapid to infuriated again in an instant. The intrusion hadn't caused him to skip a beat. "Witch," he huffed at her, and then stood and stomped back towards the drawing room.

The whole house shook as she heard him slam the door behind him. A large piece of wood fell from the stairwell, hitting the floor below with a hollow thunk.

CHAPTER 8
Foraging Forward
Day Three

The next morning, Olive forced herself not to think about her fight with Adam. She had slept in their bedroom alone that night, which she'd convinced herself was relaxing. Forcing a smile, she pulled herself out of bed and put on another musty dress and slippers before heading down to the creek to wash up. It was still dark outside, but the sun had started to peak over the horizon. She didn't hear or see Adam on her way out of the house, and she ignored the urge to search for him.

Olive rolled her eyes and pretended everything was normal again. Forcing herself to laugh off Adam's behavior from the night before, she felt happy for a moment.

She was still very hungry though, which made her feel sad again. The corn cakes had been neither substantial nor satisfying, and she hadn't eaten much anyway before Adam had gotten upset.

On their first day in the house, Olive had noticed some very ripe mulberry trees lining the front garden. She wondered if the same trees could be found mixed into the tangled brush of plants. Since it was autumn, the berries would be overripe and sparse, but they would still be sweet and refreshing. Olive would have preferred meat, milk, or something with more substance, but since she was starting to feel dizzy, mulberries would have to suffice.

As she struggled to walk through the brush in the garden, Olive realized it was much more wooded and dark than it looked from the outside. She wasn't able to navigate the space well enough to find where the mulberry trees had been, especially since it was quite early and the parts of the morning sun were still hiding behind the hills and trees. It was cold in the brush, and there were spots that were so shady from the trees that it looked closer to sunset than sunrise. Something cracked on the ground underneath one of her feet, snapping and sticking through the sole of her shoe.

"Ouch! These awful, pointless shoes!" she screeched, plopping herself down on a blanket of dried leaves to examine her foot.

Just as she was placing her slipper back on, a beam of sunlight shone through the trees above, revealing a spattering of brown, wrinkled shells.

"Walnuts!" Olive exclaimed aloud. She could see now that it had been a walnut shell that had poked through her slipper, but her foot was unscathed. She had been walking underneath a family of large walnut trees, whose large, flat leaves were the source of the shade as well as the blanket of leaves on the ground. The leaves were a happy hue of bright autumn-yellow, shading the dozens of sun-dried nuts that were scattered around Olive's place under the trees.

Gathering a dozen or so in the front of her dress, she settled down and cracked each nut open against the trunk of the tree. She ate the walnuts with excitement until her hunger had subsided, and then filled the front of her skirt with as many more as she could take with her back to the house.

The sun had risen over the house by the time she returned. It was quiet and peaceful, and the weather was crisp and sunny. She smiled as she began thinking of all the fun recipes she'd be able to make with the walnuts.

The floor rumbled as soon as she entered the house.

"Adam? Is that you?"

There was no answer.

"Adam? Are you here?"

She heard snorting around the corner, in the sitting room. Tiptoeing, she poured the walnuts from the front of her dress into a large basket she found in the dining room and peeked through the door where she'd heard the noise. Adam was hunched in the corner of the sitting room, snorting and grunting next to a large burlap bag.

"Adam, what are you doing?"

Adam looked over his shoulder at her. His face was dripping with yellow slime.

"Bleaghh!" she cried. "What is that?"

His eyes widened with embarrassment. "Eggs."

Olive began to laugh, not only because she was relieved to see Adam in a good mood, but also because she thought he looked funny with his hairy face covered in egg yolk.

"Oh, honey, would you like a cloth to clean yourself up?"

He nodded. "Could you bring me one, please?"

She returned to the front kitchen and found a musty cloth in one of the dusty cabinets, then returned to wipe the egg from his long beard and whiskers. "You even have it in your eyebrows!" she giggled as she folded the cloth and scrubbed his forehead.

"I was hungry. I went a little crazy." He blushed.

Olive wrapped her arms around his furry neck and let him nuzzle her ratty hair. She gave a comfortable sigh and brushed her head against his neck. Even in his unfortunate state, Adam still felt like the man she had fallen in love with. He was warm and soft, and she could feel the love in his embrace. He pulled her onto his lap and wrapped his arms around her shoulders. She put her arms around his waist and nuzzled his chest. The two sat motionless and silent for a long while as a feeling of warmth and calmness came over the house.

Adam spoke after a few moments. "I think you're right, Olive. I think if we just focus on moving forward, we'll be just fine. Maybe, whatever this is, it's happening to test us, to ensure we're capable of living without palace help. The sooner we show how we can fend for ourselves, the sooner everything will be back to normal."

She pulled back from her comfortable place against his chest to look at him. "What is normal, anyway, dear?" she said.

"Sidney, the way it was before," he answered. "With the palace and royalty and—"

"I'm teasing you, sweetheart." She kissed his cheek and then his lips. He shook a little and seemed nervous as he returned the kiss, and Olive thought he might cry. She kissed him harder, his furry face scratching her cheeks and chin.

"You're tickling me," she teased.

He let out a low growl as he grabbed her behind and pulled her into his lap. Straddling him, she laughed and played along, kissing his cheek and neck again.

It was then that she noticed the large burlap bag on the floor behind him, filled with several dozen more eggs.

"Adam. Where'd all those eggs come from?" She said, her voice clipped.

"Not now. Can we talk about that later?" he grumbled, burying his face in her neck.

Olive unwound herself from him and stood, gesturing at the bag. "Adam, please tell me where all these eggs came from."

"I, um— I woke up hungry last night." He started, "I was feeling angry again, too, and started craving real pancakes with butter and syrup, so I went into town in the middle of the night, and I found a bakery. I knocked on the door, and a man answered, and I, uh—told him about our situation and how hungry we were. He gave me the bag of eggs."

Olive shook her head in disbelief. "Why would a baker just *give* you several dozen eggs?" Her ears started hissing; she could tell Adam was lying to her. "I've managed a bakery. Eggs are a priceless commodity. Bakers don't just give them away like that! Did you threaten him? Did you try and scare him? What did you do?"

"No, none of that!" Adam spoke at a quick and frantic pace. "It's because he felt for us! He just wanted to help us out, that's all."

"And—how could you tell this man about all of the weird stuff that's been happening? How did you explain your appearance?"

"No, no, no! It was early this morning, when it was still dark. I stayed outside in the shadows and he only saw me for a moment. He would've thought I was crazy if I'd told him everything, so I told him we've fallen on hard times. That's all, I promise."

"Adam, a lot of people fall on hard times! We're the only ones who can't afford good food, but it's just not that easy to convince people to give away quality ingredients like fresh eggs, even to people in need." The hissing was louder again, but Olive focused on trying to keep her cool. "I find it very hard to believe that a baker would just hand these off to you so easily. Day-old bread or stale pastries, yes, even milk that's about to turn, but never eggs! Adam, I know you're lying to me!"

"No, Olive. It's just—" Adam held his head and rocked back and forth. "I, uh, I didn't want to tell you this part, but dammit! The baker told me—warned me—that the eggs were about to turn. They're only going to be good for another day or two."

The hissing in her ears halted. "Why didn't you tell me that before?" she asked.

"Yes. Just like the milk thing you just said. They're close to spoiling." He buried his head in his hands. "I told you—it's embarrassing."

"That's not embarrassing, Dear." Olive sighed with relief. "I've spent my whole life working in bakeries. I've given away imperfect food many times. I wish you'd have been honest with me before, but you don't have to feel embarrassed. You did what you had to do. You did well—and thank you."

He peeked at her from behind his hands. "Even though they're old?"

Olive waved her hand. "I worked with eggs every day at the bakery. I can smell if an egg has turned from two rooms away, and these are fine. Eggs cooked into cakes or pastries last much longer. If I bake something today, it'll last another week. This is a good thing. We're going to be just fine."

His eyes lit up. "What are you going to make?"

"It's a surprise." She winked at him and grabbed the bag of eggs and basket of walnuts before heading back to the kitchen.

It was still mid-morning, and only the third day since the night of the supermoon. It seemed so much longer than that now, but Olive felt hopeful and inspired as she set up in the kitchen to bake walnut quick-bread. She sang to herself and danced around the kitchen as she chopped walnuts, mixed ingredients, and poured batter into pans. She propped open the kitchen door so that the house filled with the aroma of spiced bread, a perfect complement to the crisp fall air.

"I wish I had some chocolate," she said to herself, remembering an old recipe she hadn't made in years.

She continued wiping the counter, perking up a second later as she remembered the chocolate she'd stashed on the windowsill outside. It had been long enough since she'd tested it, and so she decided it was safe.

The brick of chocolate sat undisturbed on the windowsill where she had left it. She made sure it was still wrapped and stashed it underneath her skirt before sneaking back into the house. She felt silly hiding it from Adam, but he had such a hard time resisting sweets. If he saw it, she was certain it wouldn't make it back to the kitchen.

Once back inside, she shut the kitchen door again and unwrapped the chocolate, cutting off a small piece for herself. It was just as smooth and delicious as she had remembered from the day before.

She'd just started working on her family's old recipe when an unsettling thought occurred to her. Once Adam discovered that the bread contained chocolate, he'd be sure to ask her where she'd gotten it. No matter what answer she gave him, she realized she ran the risk of upsetting him again. Along with Adam's unrelenting sweet-tooth, Olive had more than enough reason to keep the chocolate walnut bread a secret from him.

CHAPTER 9
Olive the Strange

"Ta-Da!" Olive waltzed into the dining room and presented Adam with a plate of sliced walnut bread.

Adam grabbed his first slice and inhaled it without a single word.

"You're welcome," she said, clearing her throat and beaming with pride.

"Thank you. It's delicious," he said.

"You are welcome, Prince Adam. And thank you."

"Prince?" He winked at her. "Let's not get carried away."

She smiled and put her arms around his neck, giving him a kiss on the cheek. He was in good spirits again.

"I'm going into town," she told him, her arms still around his neck.

"Now?" He asked. "Buy why? I want to spend time with you."

"I want to spend time with you, too, dear, and we will spend time together tonight. It'll be getting dark in a few hours, and I want to get out of the house to see if I can learn anything about what's going on with us."

"Dear, there isn't anything we can do tonight." He had taken another slice of walnut bread, and spoke between bites. "Why don't you just stay here and relax for a while?"

"I wouldn't say there's nothing we can do." She huffed. "And we'll never know if we just stay here. We have to keep living!"

Olive's ears whispered as she finished her thought.

"Living! You call this living?" Adam boomed. "You haven't stopped moving for the last three days, and still *nothing* has gotten any better. We aren't going to start living again until everything goes back to normal."

Olive shot him a dirty look, and the hissing continued. "Just moments ago, you were optimistic too, Adam. I won't let you use anger to try and keep me in the house. And things *have* gotten better. We have food because of me! We have eggs because of you! We're not starving right now because each of us went out there to be productive and provide."

His face settled, and he lifted an eyebrow at her. "Can I at least have the rest of the bread you're holding before you go?"

Sighing, she handed him the plate and kissed his cheek again. She had two loaves of chocolate walnut bread wrapped up with baker's twine against the front of her upper thighs, underneath her skirt, which was awkward and uncomfortable. She needed to head into town as soon as possible in case the knots decided to give out.

The air outside was colder than it had been earlier in the day. Olive pulled a musty blue shawl around her chest as she walked in the direction of town. By the time she reached the bottom of the hill at the edge of town, she was feeling guilty about leaving Adam at home alone. She turned towards the house back up the hill and considered heading back home to snuggle with him and a warm musty blanket. The thought of his erratic mood swings, however, forced her to keep walking.

The loaves of bread tied to her legs were another deciding factor. Her heart and mind rattled with guilt, confusion, and the newfound fear she felt of her husband as she reached the town commons. The racing thoughts caused her to panic again, leaving her dizzy and sick to her stomach.

Olive wondered if anything was ever going to feel like home again. Her husband and their brand new life together had started falling apart before they'd even had a chance to begin, and now that she'd taken a moment to let herself think about it, she doubted she would ever find or see her family again either.

She sat for a moment in despair, allowing it to center her and help her think. The reality of the situation was grim, but it was easier to feel heavy with dread than dizzy with anxiety. She stood again, directionless. She planned to head toward the tavern Jepson had told her about, but she hadn't paid attention to where he said it was located.

A woman wearing a cloak with a blue hood brushed past her.

"Excuse me, Ma'am!" Olive called. "Do you know where JB's Tavern is?"

The woman turned to meet her.

"Rose!" Olive exclaimed.

The two stared at each other, wide-eyed and speechless.

"Rose," Olive whispered. "It's so good to see a familiar face—"

"Princess—" Rose squeaked before turning away and escaping into a crowd of people at the edge of the commons.

Olive took off after her, but Rose had disappeared. Olive's ears were hissing again, and a burst of energy surged through her body. She angled her shoulder forward and charged toward the group of people.

An older man grabbed her by the shoulders. "Hey, hey! Slow down there, Missy. You're gonna hurt somebody."

She stared at the man, eyes burning. "Let me be! Do you have any idea what I've been through the past few days?"

The man laughed and forced a cheerful tone. "Well, no, I wouldn't know any of that, Miss, but I'd be happy to sit and talk with you about it. Let's sit down over here on this bale of hay, and I'll get you a nice cuppa' tea."

"Leave! Me! Alone!" she yelled at him, succumbing to the hissing in her ears.

Her eyes itched and burned as she locked gazes with the man. He stared back at her, his face dull and slack-jawed as she saw past his eyes and into his soul. His memories and insecurities began to take shape inside her mind.

She could see that he was a good man, a widowed farmer without many ill intentions. Although, she couldn't care about the good in him. He was trying to control and belittle her, which enraged her. She could see that despite the smile he wore, the man was sad. She saw blood, splintered wood, and a smattering of hay. She smelled livestock. The man was crying. The memory was recent.

The vision was gruesome, and the blood reminded her of the memory fragment of childbirth she'd seen when she'd invaded the young mother's mind. They had been standing in the same place then where she stood now with the farmer. Her thoughts wandered, and she remembered how she'd felt remorseful after leaving the woman and her children. She was no longer focused on invading the farmer's insecurities, and she wasn't angry anymore; she was sad. Her breathing slowed, and the hissing quieted and soon disappeared.

"I'm sorry about your barn," she said.

The man looked flustered and confused, but he didn't seem bothered by—or at least to have any memory of—the invasion. "So you've heard about the incident too, have you? Why thank you, but it'll all work out, I suppose." He wiped a tear from the corner of his eye. "Would you still like that cuppa' tea?"

"No, sir, but thank you very much," she said. "Can you please just tell me where JB's Tavern is?"

"Right back that way," he told her, gesturing to a road at the other end of the town commons lined with shops and street vendors. "Exit the commons to the north there and walk two blocks. When you hear the music, that'll be JB's."

"Thank you, sir." She grabbed the man's hand and shook it before trotting off in the direction of the tavern.

CHAPTER 10
Bittersweet Comfort

JB's was easy to find. Like the farmer had told her, the music gave it away. A jaunty tune filled the street outside, leading up to the double doors of the tavern. The music was unlike anything Olive had ever heard before. It was spunky and happy, like children's music, but sung in a mature, witty style like the limericks she'd heard inside the palace. The people inside JB's laughed and sang together with joy.

Olive entered through the double doors into a large, dark, smoky room that smelled of liquor and spiced tobacco. Jepson hammered away behind a grand piano in the far corner of the bar. A small crowd of men stood around him, singing along and laughing. They each held a cigar in one hand and a beer stein in the other. Three beautiful women sat together on the hood of the piano, holding cocktails and singing along to the jaunty tune, the lyrics of which Olive was close enough to hear.

"Buh—buh—Breakfast in bed! Oh, that's what she said.
But the next day she cracked an egg on my head!
She said, 'That's what you get!
You big stupid twit!
You laughed at me when I went to take a—!'"

The lyrics and piano both slowed upon the last half of the final line of lyrics. Everyone in the bar erupted in laughter, as if avoiding the word that followed was much funnier than singing it.

Olive felt awkward as she stood at the end of the bar near the door, unsure of where to stand or what to say. She watched Jepson stand up from the piano. He smiled and stretched his oversized arms above his head. Jepson was a gigantic man, and Olive felt guilty once again as she caught herself gaping at him.

One of the women sitting on the back of the piano jumped to the floor and hung her arms around Jepson's neck. He smiled and swung the girl around before placing her back on the piano and heading towards the front of the bar. The woman huffed and crossed her arms, pouting at Jepson's clear gesture of rejection.

Jepson slid over the bar top and behind the bar in one agile leap. He and the other bartender exchanged friendly conversation before Jepson walked towards the end of the bar where Olive stood. She froze.

When he spotted her, Jepson's face lit up. "Hey, Basketcase! You made it—a whole day late! Welcome."

"Um—hi." She paused, unsure how to accept the greeting. "Something came up yesterday. I wanted to make it over here last night, but I got home, and it was just one thing after another. I had to cook dinner, and that was a disaster, and then I got into an argument with—"

"Whoa, whoa, slow down there, Basketcase. It's all good. We'll get there, but let's start with a drink first. You want a drink?"

"A beer, please. A dark one, if you have it."

"Ah, a stout girl, eh? Looks like you and I will get along just fine," he said with a smile that never seemed to fade.

"I'm sorry?" she asked. "I'm not stout, am I?"

"No, I don't believe so." Jepson snickered and presented her with a glass of smooth black liquid. "It's an Irish ale. It's called a black stout."

She took the glass and sniffed it before taking a sip. It was bittersweet in a comforting way, like unsweetened cocoa mixed with fresh raspberries. "I've never had a beer like this before."

"I ordered it in from Ireland," he said, a hint of smugness in his voice.

"Well, it's lovely. Thank you." Olive took another sip and then lowered the glass to the counter. "It's Olive, by the way."

He lifted an eyebrow. "You want an olive in your beer? That's a little weird."

"No, my name," she corrected him again. "My name is Olive. Not that other thing you called me."

"Basketcase?"

"Yes, that one. That's not my name."

He let out a deep laugh that bellowed through the tavern. "I know that. You told me yesterday that your name is Olive. I just give nicknames to all my friends."

"Thank you. I'm glad you consider me to be a friend, but Basketcase doesn't sound like a very nice name to call somebody."

He sighed, looking off for a second as if he was deep in thought. "It's not supposed to be insulting. It's supposed to be fun. You gotta lighten up a bit, Olive. See Arthur over there? I call him Ashman because he smokes like a chimney. My buddy George at the other end of the bar is a sheep farmer. I call him Shithead because he smells like one."

"That sounds like a great way to make friends, Jepson. Can I call you Mr. Pig because you keep hitting on me? How do you know I'm not married?"

He shook a finger at her. "You're a spunky one, Basketcase, and I'll have you know that Mr. Pig is already taken. See, I'm not a bad guy, I just—"

Growing bored with their conversation, Olive tried to think of a way to change the subject when she remembered that she still had the loaves of walnut bread tied to her legs. She hadn't anticipated how awkward it would be to untie the trussed-up loaves in public. As Jepson continued to speak, she hiked up her skirt a little, trying to act as casual as possible and avoid letting the rest of the bar see anything they shouldn't. After finding the end of one of the strings and pulling, the first loaf of bread dropped and caught on the inside of her skirt. With the loaf cradled in fabric in the crook of her knee, she breathed in relief and did the same with the other one before she let them both fall to the ground with a thud.

Jepson raised an eyebrow to her at the sound of the falling bread. "What are you up to over there?"

Olive was embarrassed, but she played it off. "You say I'm crazy, right?"

"As a basketcase usually is."

She rolled her eyes. "Well—Basketcase just gave birth to twins."

He twisted his mouth at her and shook his head before pulling himself over the top of the bar to peer at the floor beneath Olive. He cocked his head at the sight of the loaves of wrapped bread on the floor before letting out another belly-laugh. "So many jokes I can make about that. Wow, I don't know what to say besides— bring them twins up here, Basketcase! Let's eat."

She picked up the loaves of bread and put them on the counter. "I made these with the chocolate you gave me. That's why I'm here. It's a thank-you gift."

He frowned. "That chocolate was supposed to be for you. You were supposed to eat it. I was on the way to bring it to my mother, but then I saw you. Chocolate is good for energy, and you looked like you needed it."

"I saved some for myself at home, but I wanted to bring you these. I used to run a bakery, and"—Olive sighed as she realized why she had been so eager to meet with Jepson again—"and I just miss baking for people sometimes."

Since her engagement to Adam several months earlier, Olive had baked only for him. The idea of making food for people all around to enjoy filled a warm place in her heart.

"Mmm-mmm! This bread is like cake! Real good!" Jepson's excitement brought Olive out of her thoughts. He had already cut into the bread and tasted it. "Look, lady: I have no idea how you pulled off that trick, but you can give birth all over this bar if you keep making food like this." He took another bite and called out to the other side of the bar. "Mr. Pig! Come over here and try this girl's baby bread."

She put her head in her hands. She was embarrassed by the comment and also by the way she'd presented the bread, but flattered that Jepson was enjoying it. A few moments later, a short, dark-haired man sat down on the stool next to her.

Olive's jaw dropped. "Lionel!?" she exclaimed.

Lionel gained a confused look. He looked at Jepson and then down at his lap before turning to Olive. "Uh, hello. I don't think we've met."

"Lionel, it's me, Olive Grimm. Your sister!"

He shook his head at her and then looked back at Jepson with wide eyes. Jepson shrugged and handed Lionel a hunk of bread.

"Girl's kind of a basketcase, but she makes good food. Try?" Jepson said.

Lionel took the bread from him, but did not eat it. Olive continued to stare at him.

"Lionel Grimm! Please tell me you remember me!"

He stared back at her and shrugged. "I told you already: I don't believe we've met."

"You've got to remember, brother! You know me. You were at my wedding just three days ago!" Olive's ears hissed as her frustration heightened.

"Wait… You're married?" Jepson asked.

"No," Lionel murmured. He looked down at his feet hanging off the bar stool and refused to make eye contact with her. "I have brothers. No sisters."

The hissing was infuriating inside Olive's ears now, and her temples throbbed with pain. She felt hopeless, angry, and confused. She shot Lionel a stern look, and his face went still with fear.

"Augh, shut up, not now, *not now!*" Olive screeched, closing her eyes and boxing her own ears to try and stop the hissing. The sound resonated inside her head, and pressure built up behind her eyes, making it difficult to keep them closed. She twisted the stool back so she could face the bar and leaned over the crumby, beer-soaked bar top. It hummed and vibrated against the pain and hissing inside her head.

"Did she wear her hair like that at her wedding?" Lionel asked Jepson, disregarding Olive's apparent frustration.

His comment was all but drowned out by the hissing and humming inside her head, and it enraged her.

How dare he be so disrespectful! An oily voice sounded, joining the hissing.

She smacked her ears again, over and over while she hummed aloud. "Stop it! Stop it! Stop it!"

"Wow, is she okay?" Lionel asked Jepson.

"She's alright. Just a little nutty. Nothing these walls haven't seen a hundred and one times before. I'll be around to keep an eye on her," Jepson informed him. "Try that bread. Damn good."

Listen to them ignoring you. You're no better than a common drunk to your own brother! The oily voice continued through the hissing, and Olive felt as if she was floating further away from her seat at the bar. She could still hear the two men's voices becoming quieter and trailing off with each passing moment.

"What if she poisoned it?" Lionel asked, quieter still.

"Oh, you know you'd eat it anyway, Pig. You love dessert!" Jepson retorted.

"And what if it's drugged?" Lionel's voice continued to spiral into the distance.

"Now that you mention it, I feel great!"

Both men chuckled, their voices low and echoing until Olive couldn't hear anything at all. Even the hissing sound was gone.

She was conscious of her body sitting on the barstool in the tavern. When she opened her eyes, though, Olive could see that she was alone in an empty room with stark white walls, and she was standing, though her knees still carried the sensation of being bent.

The room was cold, though the tavern was warm; she could feel both temperatures in separate parts of her consciousness. The lights inside the white room were so bright that she had to squint, but there was no telling how big the room was.

The cold, sterile feel of the room was nerve-wracking. Olive tried to hold on to the warmer reality of the tavern, but soon that, too, began drifting away. The harder she tried to wake up, the fainter the feeling of the warm tavern became, and the more the stark whiteness solidified around her.

All she could see was the bright light as she peered around the room, though she could feel something watching her and began hearing a faint hissing throughout the room. She tried crying out for help, but her screams were silent.

"You think she's a witch?" Lionel's voice echoed once again, from somewhere high above the room.

Olive tried to call out to him, but again, her voice was silent.

The sound of the two men laughing at Lionel's remark drifted into oblivion, and the hiss grew louder and bounced off one bright, white wall to the next. The sounds multiplied, slithering around the room until they centered behind Olive's right ear. She turned her head towards the sound with caution.

A shiny black figure loomed against the white wall behind her. She gave a silent gasp at what appeared, to be a large water snake. It was longer than she was tall, as thick as her upper arm. The snake gave a menacing hiss, floating and slithering around behind her as if it was swimming in water. Soon, it slithered in front of her, staring at her with intense yellow eyes.

The snake hovered in front of her for several torturous seconds. Olive could not move. She could not even open her mouth to try and scream. It stared into her, past her eyes and into her soul. It was invasive and angry, the same way Olive had acted towards the young mother and the farmer in the commons. Her mind went white and cold as the snake fed on her innermost thoughts and memories.

Finally, it began to speak. "You hated being a princess."

She tried to tell it that it was wrong, but her lips and eyes were frozen still.

The snake continued. "This is pretty fun for you, isn't it, dear? Running amuck like a peasant child instead of the good little princess you're expected to be. You're nothing but a dreadful, chaotic renegade!"

The snake's words were somewhat true, she realized. There was no doubt that what was happening was terrible. Yet, in the short time since the night of the supermoon, Olive had started to enjoy the freedom to explore and learn her new surroundings, no matter how weird it all was. The weeks she'd spent being waited on by servants in the palace were dull and boring: having people dress her and do her hair, cook her food, and even salt it for her. She'd once told Adam that her days in the palace had felt longer, which he'd accepted as a good thing.

At one point, days before the wedding, she remembered being so under-stimulated during a shoe sizing that she'd imagined a violent storm flooding the Land of Sidney. In the daydream, she and the rest of the royal family and palace servants had rushed into town to gather the commoners and bring them back to the palace for safety. There, they had fed and housed the town until the flooding subsided, at which point they had all worked together to repair the damage from the storm and rebuild the town stronger and more beautiful.

Now, Olive cringed at the memory.

"It's selfish, really." The snake hissed between sentences. "You wished for a storm, and then dreamt of it, and now look what's happened. I'll bet you're wondering now if you could be the one who caused it, but you're also doubting your or anyone's ability to do so."

Olive tried to shake her head in denial, but she was frozen in place, still unable to move or speak.

"Oh, but of course you don't." The snake shook its head. "Because you haven't thought about that, or even cared that you may be at all responsible. You've just been *so* concerned with how much fun all of this is for you that you've forgotten what's important. You've forgotten about your husband at home."

The snake raised its tail up to its head and used it like a hand to rub its brow. Its tail then drifted towards the lock of matted hair against Olive's right temple. It tugged on the lock and moved closer to examine it.

"Now, where did you learn to style your hair this way?" The snake gave a maniacal cackle as it teased her.

The feel of the snake's cold, scaly tail against Olive's cheek and neck sent a wave of nausea throughout her entire body. Its tail fell from her cheek and then reappeared in front of her a moment later, curled around the handle of a hand mirror. The mirror held a moving image of Adam, as furry and unkempt as ever. He was in his drawing room, howling in pain. He looked miserable.

"You stupid woman. You witch!" the snake hissed. "Just look what you've done to him!"

Olive had heard enough. She was not a witch. She knew she had nothing to do with the strange happenings after the supermoon. She loved Adam despite his flaws, and she would stand by him. It took most of her strength, but with a surge of fierce adrenaline, Olive forced herself to close her eyes so the snake could no longer hold her with its stare. The back of her eyelids burned, and her ears throbbed and crackled with agony. Olive gritted her teeth against the pain but managed to keep her eyelids closed.

The snake screeched in front of her, and she lunged towards the sound. Continuing to keep her eyes closed, she grabbed the snake below its head with one hand, gripping its body with her other. She squeezed and twisted to disengage it, then dug her nails into its scales until she felt flesh ripping in her palms.

She kept her eyes closed the whole time, but could hear the snake hissing and screeching as it tried to slither out of her hold. She held on tight, twisting and digging while her eyes continued to burn behind her eyelids.

Finally, the snake stopped screeching, and its body went limp. The burning behind her eyes softened, and a cool, soothing feeling set in. She opened them to find the snake lying lifeless on the floor of the white room.

"Wow! This bread tastes like cake!"

The happy sound of Lionel's voice sounded throughout the white room, which began to fade from view as the mirror behind the bar reemerged in front of her. "It's similar to a dessert bread my mother used to make when I was a kid! She used to call it—something. Something funny."

Olive was back in the bar with nothing of the white room around her now, nor an inkling of hissing. She could see and hear that it was Lionel who was speaking.

"Nutty brunette," she mumbled.

"Aw, look who's awake!" Jepson cooed. "And yes, you are a nutty brunette. I ain't changing your nickname, though."

Olive looked around the bar. She patted her cheeks and inspected each hand for wounds.

"Was I asleep?" she asked.

Jepson chuckled. "You, uh, kind of freaked out there. Took one sip of your beer and passed out five minutes ago. Can't handle your stout, I see."

Olive looked at the dark beer that was still almost full in front of her, then back at her hands, and then over at Lionel, who was side-eyeing her.

"How did you know about that?" he asked her.

"Know about what?" Olive had all but forgotten the words she'd spoken just moments earlier.

"Nutty brunette." Lionel was leering at her now. "How do you know about nutty brunette cake? I used to eat that when I was a kid."

"Nutty brunette is an old French recipe," she lied, not wanting to upset or confuse Lionel any further. "You said your mother used to call this bread something funny, but you couldn't remember what that was."

Lionel cocked his head at her and then crossed his arms, frowning.

Olive huffed and looked at her feet, embarrassed and ashamed that she had continued to upset him.

Jepson smacked his hands on the bar top to take back their attention. "Who wants another drink?"

"I have to go home—to my husband. It's getting late," Olive said.

Jepson and Lionel shot each other a comical glance before Jepson looked back at her. "Okay there, Basketcase. You go home to your new husband."

He was mocking her, but she didn't care. After returning from her vision of the white room with the snake, she was exhausted in body, mind, and spirit. For the first time since the night of the supermoon, she looked forward to going home to her decrepit house to be with Adam. She wanted him to hold her and to tell her everything would be okay, but most of all, she wanted to sleep.

Having little strength to say much more, she gave a sheepish wave to the two men without saying another word and made her way to the front doors of the tavern.

"Hey, Basketcase!" Jepson called from behind her.

She stopped in the tavern doorway but did not turn to him. She could barely keep her eyes open, fighting to keep herself upright. She was in a hurry to get outside, where the air was cool and fresh.

Jepson continued. "One of your, eh—dread-y things is loose."

She didn't look back or say anything more. She only reached up to touch the side of her head. Even in her state of delirious exhaustion, she gasped and then smiled upon feeling what Jepson was talking about. One of her matted locks had once again become a smooth, soft curl.

"Adam! Adam! Come quick!" shouted Olive, who had run all the way from JB's Tavern. She came bursting through the double front doors of the house with a smile on her face and hope in her heart. Minutes earlier, she had been exhausted enough to fall asleep underneath a tree, but now she was full of energy and excitement.

"Adam! Look what happened, dear! It's a miracle!" She skipped down the hallway leading to the west wing and pounded on the drawing room door with both hands.

"Well, hello!" Adam's voice came from behind her.

She turned around. She could see that Adam had washed up. His long beard was neatly tied, and so was the hair on his head. He had changed his shirt, and though it was still mildewed and yellow, Olive found her husband to look very handsome. He stood with confidence, eating a thick slice of walnut bread.

"Oh, Adam! You look so nice! I'm so glad you're up and about." She wrapped her arms around his neck as he squeezed her behind.

She smiled and pulled herself further into Adam's embrace. He nuzzled her neck and twirled her around so he could envelop her against the corner of the hallway. They kissed, and Adam unbuckled his belt. Olive's breath was heavy with excitement. She closed her eyes and tilted her head against the wall as she waited for more. He stared at her for just a moment more before he made his move. Olive could feel his pent-up frustration converting to pleasure for them both as she gave into the sensations of the cathartic romping.

Sometime later, the pair fell into a deep, comfortable sleep on a large sofa in the sitting room. Olive lay on Adam's chest, and Adam rested his large, furry hands against the small of her back. The sound of his breathing against her ear comforted her as she slept.

CHAPTER 11
More Questions than Answers
Day Four

Olive dreamt about the house being clean and stable once again. Natural light flooded every room, and the furniture throughout the house was simple and pretty in shades of pale pink and lacy white. A gaggle of chickens clucked and around a garden to the side of the house, which was overflowing with fat red tomatoes and a variety of other vegetables. Bright purple and orange carrots poked out of the ground in several places, yielding a fountain of bushy, vibrant green carrot tops.

A pair of sheep trotted to Olive's side from somewhere behind the house. They stopped so she could pet their soft woolen coats and bleated in a sing-song way as they circled back behind the house. The air smelled of fresh apples and tulip petals, and Olive hummed a happy tune as she settled down under a walnut tree at the edge of the lawn. The thick brush was gone, and she could see all of Sidney again from her place underneath the tree.

Peering back towards the house, she expected to find a dashing, clean-shaven Adam walking out the front door. He didn't show, but she was confident that he'd be joining her soon. She continued to hum to herself as she waited, but the sound of the song she hummed soon changed. The playful tune turned darker, as did the sky.

"Adam?" she called. She stopped humming, but the ominous tune still sounded in the air as the wind whipped through the trees above. She crossed her arms over her chest to fight the chill, and as she stood, her legs shook.

"Adam?" she called again, her voice hoarse and weak.

The wind was strong, and it whipped at her feet and legs, but just as she was about to fall over, she jolted awake. She was still safe and warm on the sofa in the sitting room, but she was alone.

Through the window behind the sofa, she could see that it was still quite dark, though the sun was beginning to peek out from the horizon. The room spun a bit as she sat up. Her whole body was sore, a gentle reminder of her misadventures from the day before. She massaged her throbbing temples and sore neck, wincing as the details about Lionel, the white room, the snake, and everything else flooded back to her. As she moved her hand forward again from her neck back to her temple, she brushed the soft curl she'd discovered the night before. She smiled, realizing she hadn't even gotten to show Adam. She doubted he had noticed on his own, but was excited all over again to show him, especially now that he was feeling positive once again.

Olive decided to start her day early. She didn't see or hear Adam anywhere inside or around the house, so she ate a quick breakfast from her secret stash of nutty brunette bread and then washed up by the creek before getting dressed. In her dressing room, she noticed that her clothing and shoes didn't smell as musty as they had the day before, although she may have grown accustomed to the smell.

She pulled the curl from the back of her head forward so she could inspect it in the full-length mirror. There was no indication that it had been matted like the rest of the hair on her head, which continued to prove itself impossible to untangle by hand.

She headed out towards the town just as daylight broke. Sidney was peaceful and quiet during the early morning hours. There was a chill in the air, but it wasn't windy or unpleasant, and the town commons were empty. Olive sat down on a hay bale and told herself it was okay to relax. Everything was starting to look up for her and Adam. She took a deep breath in and a deep breath out, and then another, but stopped short on the third round as she remembered the debacle that had gone down in the commons the day before.

"Rose," she huffed, remembering how Rose had started to call her 'Princess'. Even Lionel, her own brother, hadn't remembered Olive, yet it was clear Rose had. Rose had acted afraid when she saw Olive, too.

Olive was no longer relaxed. She knew she had to find Rose.

"Hello?! Is anyone there?"
Olive returned to the metal fence surrounding the large white house where she'd once known the palace to be. There was no one in sight to hear her calling out, and the fence surrounding the property was much too tall for her to climb over. Out of desperation, she found a large stick and began to clank it against the fence to gain the attention of someone inside.

"Let me in, please!" she yelled, knowing full-well that her behavior was inappropriate.

Soon, a stocky brown-haired man carrying gardening shears danced his way to the gate. He was humming a playful tune and beaming.

"Mr. Curtis!" she blurted. "I'm so glad you remember me!"

Mr. Curtis kept smiling but twitched one eye in a confused manner. "Remember you from where, ma'am?"

She covered her face and huffed before making eye contact once again. "It's nothing. May I speak with the king? I mean the—the prime leader?"

He cocked his head and twisted his lips. "I assume you mean the head counselor, ma'am?"

"Yes, him. The head counselor." She nodded.

Mr. Curtis nodded back.

"Thank you, Mr. Curtis. Thank you. May I speak with him?"

Mr. Curtis continued to smile, but shook his head. "No, ma'am."

She huffed again. "Why not?"

His smile faded a bit. "Because, ma'am, there are rules. I can't just let anyone into the House of Counsel. Why are you here? What is your business? If you'd like to wait, I can give word to the head counselor's secretary, and she will speak with him. Then he can decide whether to meet with you or not."

She sighed. "I wonder if *you* can help me, then. I'm here to ask about one of his servants. I mean, I think she's a servant here. She used to be. It's complicated."

His eyes narrowed. "A servant? At the House of Counsel? I'm afraid you're mistaken, dear."

She ran her hands over her matted hair. "Yes, the cooks, the seamstresses. Even you, Mr. Curtis, as a gardener."

Mr. Curtis chuckled, his smile returning. "Yes, there are plenty of diligent workers and assistants here in the House of Counsel. But no, ma'am. Sidney isn't a land of royalty or servitude. Do you know someone who is keeping servants illegally? Is that why you'd like to speak with the head counselor?"

Olive shook her head. "I apologize, sir. I, um—I'm not from around here. I am hoping, though, that I might visit with a friend while I'm here. I think she might work with you in the House of Counsel. A seamstress called Rose. Do you know her?"

He nodded his head with vigor and grinned. "Oh, yes! Rose is Head Lady Jeanne Beaumont's personal tailor. She's a very talented girl. You said she's a friend of yours?"

"Yes, sir," said Olive, looking at her feet. "Or, she *was* a friend of mine. We had a feud, but I'd like to speak with her again, if possible."

Mr. Curtis's smile softened. "That's very kind of you to want to patch up your friendship with a nice girl like Rose, but I'm afraid she isn't here yet. It's still quite early, ma'am. Why are you out and about all by yourself? The sun has only just risen."

Olive nodded. "Will you please just let me know when I might be able to come back and see her?"

"Oh, of course, ma'am. Didn't mean to pry. Rose will be here in just a few hours. Should I let her know you came around looking for her?"

"No!" Olive shouted before composing herself and continuing on. "Please don't tell her I was here. I'd rather not have her know I'm in town just yet. Our last meeting was a bit unpleasant, and I wouldn't want to cause her unnecessary nerves ahead of time."

"Oh, of course, ma'am. Won't say a word." Mr. Curtis pantomimed locking his lips closed.

CHAPTER 12
True Colors

"Basketcase! Boy, am I glad to see you!" Jepson popped his head out from underneath the bar, where he was rustling through cabinets and making a great deal of noise.

"Really?" Olive asked him as she walked into the empty tavern after leaving the House of Counsel. "I didn't expect to find you here this early. I was hoping to meet with a friend, but I wasn't able to find her, so I went for a walk and saw the tavern doors were open." The familiar clanking of metal bowls echoed from behind the bar. "That's, uh, quite a lot of dishes I hear over there." She cringed. "You can hear it all the way from the road. I came in to ask if you needed some help."

Jepson stood, brushing off his crisp white shirt and black apron. "Your ears must have been ringing."

"I'm sorry?" Olive said, cupping her hands over her ears.

"Relax, Basketcase. It's an expression." He rolled his eyes. "It means I was hoping you'd come by today. I was planning to mention it to Lionel when he gets here. Didn't you say you used to manage a bakery?"

She nodded.

"So does that mean you know how to decorate a cake?"

She nodded again. "It was one of my favorite things to do."

Jepson shook a triumphant fist in the air. "It's my mother's birthday today, and I'm in charge of getting the cake. Lionel's family's business has the best food in Sidney, but for some reason they don't have anyone who knows how to do cake decorating."

"It's almost like they had someone and forgot she existed." She snorted and rolled her eyes.

"Lionel's heading over now with the cake and some decorating supplies. We were going to attempt to do it ourselves, just Lionel and I, but now that you're here…"

"Now that I'm here, you and Lionel want to take credit for my artistic genius?"

"So, you'll help?" His eyes lit up.

She chuckled and threw her hands into the air. "I'd love to."

"Fantastic. Hey, Mr. Pig! Basketcase is going to help us decorate!"

Lionel entered the tavern carrying a tall white box and a burlap bag. On a large table near the window at the front of the tavern, Jepson laid out some large metal trays and an old tablecloth he'd procured from behind the bar. The burlap sack Lionel had brought contained several tins of frosting, small bottles of colorful flavored liqueurs, and a variety of decorating tools. The two men examined the tools, making confused and humorous expressions on purpose. Olive laughed from the barstool near the table, where she'd been sitting while the men spread out to organize their workspace.

"What are you doing laughing by yourself over there? Come help us, Basketcase," Lionel teased.

"I thought you didn't like me?" she teased back. "I was staying out of the way."

"I think you're odd and a little creepy, but I never said I didn't like you," he retorted.

She smiled and jumped off the barstool to join them. "So, what do we want the cake to look like?"

"Something simple on the top. Just 'Happy Birthday, Jeanne' and some framing around the words. The sides here, though—" Jepson pointed to the three layers of bare yellow cake held together by sticky white frosting—"that's the part where we have to be creative. Do you have any ideas?"

She held a finger to her lips and examined the sides of the cake. "It'll come to me."

She set Jepson and Lionel to work portioning the frosting and setting up the tools while she spread a base layer of white icing over the entire cake. It felt a lot like a day back at the bakery, which made it easier for her to settle and relax.

"So, Jepson," Olive said. "Your mother's name is Jeanne. Can you tell me about your family?"

Jepson chuckled. 'I'm never quite sure what to say about my family. My mother's an amazing woman who raised a spoiled brat only-child by the name of— me. My father is a stuckity old politician who thinks he owns Sidney."

"And why is it that he thinks he owns Sidney?" she asked, adding a layer of pearl-colored frosting on top of the base coat.

"Because he thinks that being Head Counselor makes him King, or something."

She stopped icing the cake and stared at him. "So your mother *is* Lady Jeanne? And your father is the head counselor?"

"Unfortunately." Jepson scoffed.

"So, you're a bit like royalty, then?" she asked.

He shook his head. "Not at all."

Olive pursed her lips, pausing to grab a plate of orange frosting to begin icing the top of the cake. She looked back at Jepson again. "But you live in the House of Counsel, correct? You grew up there? And you're an only child, so won't you be Head Counselor next?"

He laughed and shook his head again. "No, Basketcase. That's not how it works. Who told you all that?"

She huffed. "I'm sorry. It's just that where I used to live, we had a palace and a royal monarchy."

Jepson shook his head. "Where the hell were you living?"

"Yeah, where'd we grow up, sis?" Lionel teased, struggling to fill a pastry bag with light yellow frosting. "Enlighten me."

"Don't be rude, Pig," Jepson snapped, drowning a bowl of frosting in a pool of bright green liqueur. "Damnit, this green is a bit boozy now."

Olive, thankful for the natural change in subject, laughed aloud as she wiped the excess liqueur that had spilled onto the table. "That's okay. We can keep it. I can still use it sparingly to do touch-ups at the end. By the way, what is your father's name? I want to know what to call him if I see him around town."

"His name is James Beaumont. As a commoner, though, you must always make sure to refer to him as Counselor Beaumont."

"Beaumont? So that's your name. Jepson Beaumont. JB's Tavern is your initials."

"Nah, I didn't name JB's after myself. I named it after my mother."

"It looks like you named JB's after everyone in your family," Olive teased, moving her icing work to the top of the cake.

"She's right, Jep." Lionel laughed under his breath.

"Shut it, Pig. You know my father can't stand this place."

"Why does he hate it, though?" Olive asked. "I can understand someone not wanting to come here. I mean, it smells like smoke, and it can get a bit loud. But you're his only son, and you're running a successful business. He should be proud of you."

Jepson rubbed his temples in frustration. "The man has always been a politician, even before he was Head Counselor. My mom nearly died while giving birth to me, and so they never had any more children. My dad felt I needed to carry on his political legacy, but all I wanted to do was write music."

"So, you opened a tavern?" Olive asked.

He pointed to the piano at the other end of the bar. "A tavern with music. Being a professional pianist isn't lucrative, at least not with the type of music I play. I found a way to make do, though, and people love it."

"I heard you playing yesterday when I came in," she told him. "I've never heard music like that before. It's fun and unique. What do you call it?"

"I don't know," he shrugged. "They're just old limericks, for the most part. I change the words, add piano music, and then practice until it becomes part of me."

"I enjoyed what little I heard before. You have a real gift, Jepson," she said as she used a paintbrush and sculpting tool to add tiny details to one side of the cake. "Can you play us a little something right now?"

Jepson's eyes lit up, and he twirled out of his chair into a standing position. In an almost theatrical manner, he pointed at the piano near the back of the bar with both of his massive arms. "I can never turn down a request like that!"

He began humming and dancing with an invisible partner as he made his way across the floor to the piano. He spun in a wide circle before planting himself at the bench, acting as if he were overcome with dizziness. Olive laughed aloud, and Lionel rolled his eyes and snickered as they focused their attention on Jepson's one-man show.

He started with a catchy opening riff that was peppy and fun. He repeated it several times before changing it up and letting the melody continue. He opened his lips a few times as if he were about to sing something, but then he laughed instead and continued playing jovial tunes. It was clear after the first few times that the promise of him singing was meant as a tease. The song was goofy, fun, and all piano.

Olive hopped up from the table and began dancing a sort of jig in an open area in front of the piano. Jepson saw her and sped up the tempo, and she rolled her eyes and began to dance faster to keep up. She gestured for Lionel to join her, but he crossed his arms and shook his head.

"Oh, but come on, dear brother!" Olive called, not caring in the moment about how they'd probably make fun of her later for saying so. She twirled over to his seat and grabbed his arms to pull him onto the dance floor. After a few moments of Olive's coercing, a reluctant Lionel stood and joined her. He danced as far away from her as he could, looking at the floor as he tapped his feet in a small circle.

The music stopped as Jepson slammed his fists onto as many keys as possible. "What the devil, Lionel! Why won't you dance with the lady?"

Lionel threw his hands above his head. "Maybe I just don't want to dance with my sister!"

There was a moment of confused silence before Olive let out a relieved breath. "So, you do remember?"

He shot her a pointed look. "No, I don't. Not at all. It's just that you say all these weird things, and you put it in my head that I'm supposed to treat you like my sister, and I just—I can't dance with you, okay?"

Jepson spoke up. "Hold on. Pig? Is something else going on with you? You've been out of sorts all morning."

He huffed and rubbed his brow. Then he walked back to the table to sit down. "Yeah. I was trying not to think about it, but there's something pretty awful going on at home."

"Well, what is it?" Jepson asked.

He sniffled and settled on a nearby barstool, sweeping a tear from one of his eyes. "My, uh, family's dairy cow died last night. I know she was just a dumb cow, but she's been around since I was a kid. She wasn't just a pet. She was like part of the family."

Olive gasped. "Caramel!"

Lionel looked at her with dagger eyes. "Stop following me, will you?"

Olive pursed her lips. "Please tell us what happened?"

"She was slaughtered." He choked out the words, his voice high as he held back tears.

"I'm so sorry, Pig." Jepson stood up from his seat at the piano and started toward the table where Lionel was sitting. "That's awful, awful news."

"You know, it could have been worse," Lionel continued. "Caramel was getting older. Someone was going to have to do it soon, either way. It's just terrible because it's scary, you know? Brutal. She was just massacred. I don't like knowing she had to suffer."

"It is a big deal, though." Jepson's eyes were serious. "After what happened to Ol' Farmer Ruthers' chicken coop, this is only going to keep happening."

"Chicken coop?" Olive asked, "I met a nice old farmer yesterday who I think had lost some livestock."

Jepson turned to Olive. "Everyone in Sidney is on edge right now. Ol' Farmer Ruthers is one of the kindest men in Sidney. Wouldn't hurt a soul. The man woke up yesterday morning to find his chicken coop torn apart! The barn, the chickens—everything was just in shambles."

"I walked past Ruthers' Farm this morning," Lionel shuddered. "There's still blood and feathers everywhere."

"What's peculiar, though," Jepson continued, "is that Ruthers said there were bones and chicken feet everywhere, but not a single egg left was left behind. The fucker ate 'em all, shells and everything."

Lionel's pale skin turned a tinge of green as he covered his mouth with his hand.

Olive gasped. A dozen thoughts raced through her head: Adam's nocturnal behavior, his sketchy story about the baker, all those eggs, and how they had smelled so fresh and not at all like they were about to turn—

"Why don't you head home, Pig?" Jepson patted his friend on the back as he spoke in a calming tone. "Thanks for bringing everything over. I'll come and fetch you before the party tonight."

Lionel nodded but looked at the floor and said nothing as he slid off the barstool and headed towards the front door. As Jepson walked Lionel out, Olive wobbled back into a chair. Her hands and shoulders shook, which she feared she couldn't hide from Jepson while sitting. She stood again but began pacing near the piano.

"Whoa, Basketcase. gonna change your nickname to Fidget. Why so jumpy?" Jepson asked as he walked back towards her.

"I'm just, um—worried about the farmer," she said, trying to evade the panic in her voice. "I met him, like I said. He seemed upset. Do they know who did it?"

"Who?" Jepson turned to her; his eyes narrowed. "No, Basketcase, nobody knows *what* did it. Whatever it is, though, the chaos is left behind is more than just a common wolf or two could pull off. This is something big; something beastly."

"But what if it's not a beast," she sputtered, sounding a bit more abrupt than intentioned. "What if it's just something sad?"

"No sane creature would slaughter the way this thing does," he continued. "The thing is diseased or crazed in some way. It needs to be found, and it needs to be killed before it hurts anything else."

As her thoughts continued to race, Olive panicked. Graphic visions of her family pet being tortured by her husband raced through her mind, followed by the equally terrible thought of Jepson and the townspeople hunting and killing her husband. The visions became almost real for a moment, welcoming back the familiar hiss inside her ears.

"No, no, *no!*" she screeched as the hissing grew louder. Slamming her hands against her throbbing temples over and over again, she fell to her knees on the tavern floor, swaying and humming as she begged her nerves to keep calm.

Jepson knelt next to her. "Basket—Olive!" he shouted, shaking her shoulders. "What the hell is going on with you?"

"Nothing! No! I don't know! Leave me alone!"

"Olive, God dammit, look at me!"

She gritted her teeth and moved her hands away from her face so she could look at Jepson straight-on. Her eyes burned with fury as she let out a high-pitched roaring screech. The emotion fell from Jepson's face as the blank look of stillness set in.

Olive's eyes kept still against Jepson's dumb expression. The visions of Jepson slaughtering Adam played over and over in the back of her mind, soon solidifying so she could almost see it happening in the space between her and Jepson. One of Jepson's eyes twitched, as if he was trying to blink. Olive fumed, staring further into him.

"Don't you dare," Olive hissed. "You will never hurt my husband." Their eyes locked once again and Olive let the hissing sound consume her. The feeling was becoming all too familiar now, and this time she welcomed it with a smirk.

Olive's piercing stare tunneled past Jepson's eyes and into his soul. She could see all his darkest thoughts and deepest insecurities. She could see and feel his memories: that time he'd stolen from his father's coin collection, his superficial journey from scrawny child to buff, overgrown adult—a lifetime of recollections. Most of Jepson's buried memories were humorous, not offensive, and nothing seemed harsh enough to use against him.

Then she saw it: the one insecurity she could use to destroy the man who wanted to kill her husband. It was scandalous and illogical, and she knew that in a place like Sidney, it would ruin his reputation. This secret, although it could be catastrophic for Jepson if revealed, had been particularly difficult for Olive to find. It wasn't hidden in his consciousness, but it also wasn't buried in his insecurities. Rather, Jepson had kept the secret for years as a consistent part of his private life. It was only the perceptions of others that forced him to keep it tucked away.

"Fff—" she hissed. Her lips formed the cruel words she would need to overtake him, but before she

started speaking, she shut her mouth again. The fury in her heart subsided and was replaced with confusion. Even in her state of concentrated anger, despite her will to save Adam, Olive realized she could not sabotage Jepson. He had helped and befriended her, and he'd done the same for others.

But words were already creeping back upon her tongue. She found that she couldn't look away from Jepson, even if she wanted. Without her consent, her lips once again formed the first syllable of the word. A slow and inaudible groan crept up through her teeth, and her jaw felt as if she were biting into a slab of wood as she clenched down again.

She breathed through her nose and hummed to keep her lips closed and the word at bay. Then, with a surge of strength, Olive closed her eyes.

There was blackness, followed by an intense light she could see and feel even though her eyes were still closed. She heard nothing besides the sound of her own breath.

Olive kept her eyes shut and breathed in and out. She continued to hum in a low tone, trying to catch the attention of whatever might be in the room with her. She pressed her tongue against her teeth and blew to create a hissing sound. "Come out, come out, wherever you are, you little shit," she taunted.

There was silence. Then someone tapped her on the shoulder. Olive spun around, opening her eyes to find she was again face-to-face with the snake in the white room.

"I thought I killed you," she sputtered.

The snake cackled in the voice of an older woman. "No no, you little bitch! You killed my dear brother."

"What is it you want from me? How many of you are there?"

"Oh, I think you know those answers already, my dear." The snake used its tail to tug at one of the three remaining pieces of matted hair around Olive's head.

Olive furrowed her eyebrows and shook her head so that the lock of hair fell from the snake's grip. "What must I do to get rid of you?"

The snake cackled again and let out a rough cough, ignoring the question. "So that friend of yours. Some secret, eh?"

Olive swallowed hard. "Jepson's secret doesn't mean anything."

"Oh, you don't say!" the snake shouted. "You should have seen the look on your face when you realized the big news. You were devastated."

"I was only confused," she answered. "It doesn't make any sense."

"You naïve child! The whole thing makes an awful lot of sense! All the signs are there. You just don't want to believe it."

"Why wouldn't I? Jepson's personal life doesn't affect me at all."

"*Au contraire, ma belle.* Wasn't your plan to use it as blackmail? After all, Jepson wants to slaughter your—sorry, but what is Adam these days? A bear? A dog? *A beast?*"

"You bitch!" Olive tried to close her eyes, but the snake stared into her, forcing her to keep her eyes open and the rest of her body still.

"You were flattered when you thought he was coming onto you, weren't you? Even in your hideous state, you thought that maybe he *liked* you, did you not? But now you see that you're just another one of his pity-friends—a charity case, if you will. He treats everyone the same special way he's treated you. Oh, how could you be so self-centered, dear?"

The snake peered deep into her eyes in a way that made her feel very weak. "It must be heartbreaking to find out that you were once a very beautiful young woman, and now people see your face and feel afraid. Your own brother won't even dance with you. You must feel like such an *ugly* little witch!"

The snake raised her tail back into Olive's line of sight, revealing the hand mirror once more. In its face, Olive could see a vision of Adam. He was naked, his whole body covered with thick, raggedy fur. The fury on his face was glossed over by a smirk of content as he feasted on a shrieking, crying cow. Caramel.

"Take it away!" Olive pleaded, her eyes and body stiff. "Please, I want to close my eyes!"

She tried to cover her face, but her arms were heavy against her sides, and she could not move them. Big, fat tears welled in her eyes. Wailing in despair and anger, tears poured down her cheeks and onto her chest, thick and plentiful and clouding her vision. Soon, the tears distorted the view of the snake in front of her. Her eyelids swelled, each sob catching in her throat until she gasped for air. She coughed, gagged, and dry-heaved until she could no longer breathe.

The gagging grew louder and more intense until Olive realized she could breathe again. She could still hear the coughing and hacking in front of her, though it was no longer her making the sounds. Her breathing steadied and her vision cleared, and though her eyes were sore and a bit clouded still, she could see and move her arms and neck. On the floor below her, the snake lay belly up. It was gasping for air and hacking and coughing the same way Olive had been moments earlier.

"You witch! You did this to me!" The snake's voice was raspy and pained.

"You made me cry," Olive giggled upon realizing what had happened. "I couldn't close my eyes, but you *let* me cry. I couldn't see you through my tears, and so you couldn't hold onto me."

The snake lay motionless at her feet. Olive smirked at it and shook her head before shutting her eyes to think of happier memories.

She thought about a time in her childhood when Lionel had baked Christmas cookies, using salt instead of sugar by mistake. Olive had tasted the dough after he'd mixed it and let him know it was much too salty, but Lionel hadn't listened, deciding to make the cookies anyway. Olive had relished in a wave of I-told-you-so's later in the day, and then she and Lionel had spent the evening singing Christmas carols and labeling the family's kitchen containers.

Olive giggled aloud at the memory as the smell of stale smoke and whiskey flooded back to her. She was in the tavern again, where Jepson lay passed out across from her on the bare floor. His breathing was steady, but he wasn't awake.

"Wake up, Jep!" She shook him a bit, but he didn't stir.

She stood, and a chill of uneasiness ran up her spine. She was tired again, the same as she'd been after her last run-in with the snake, but she could not return home to face Adam after what she had seen in the snake's mirror. An amalgam of conflicting feelings ran over her. Her eyelids were heavy, and she found it difficult to stand upright.

Stumbling, she grabbed a faded tablecloth from one of the tavern tables and used it like a blanket to cover Jepson on the floor. Then she grabbed another one for herself, slipping into a large booth where she could lie on her side along the cushioned seat. As she began to drift to sleep, Olive glanced once more at Jepson, who showed no apparent signs of distress. It was then that she noticed the cake they had decorated a few feet behind him on the table. The cloudiness of exhaustion made the memory of decorating it seem like such a long time ago.

It was also difficult for her to remember why she'd decorated the cake as she had. She was both proud and bewildered by the design she'd created. A splattering of small yellow and blue stars danced throughout a celestial icing storm covering the tall, layered sides of the cake. Wisps of blue and green mimicked wind and water throughout the scenery of a night sky. The round top layer of the cake was frosted in pale orange, resembling a full moon.

Olive forced a small smile. "You're not bad luck anymore, Supermoon. I forbid it," she whispered. "I order you to be good luck for me."

And with that, she continued whispering positive, encouraging words to herself until her mind went blank and she drifted off.

CHAPTER 13
Jealousy

Olive could hear her heartbeat pulsing in her ears, and feel it pounding through all four of her limbs when she woke up a few hours later. It was dark, and she'd been startled awake by something, though she couldn't remember where she was until her knee hit the table next to the booth where she lay.

"Jepson?" she called. "Are you awake?"

"Who is he?!" she heard Adam shout.

"Adam?" she breathed, her temples and neck stiffening with panic.

"Who is he, Olive?" Adam gruffed from somewhere nearby.

"Adam, where are you? I didn't feel well. I've been asleep." She squinted to see Adam's hunched silhouette lumbering towards her.

"You've been gone all day and half the night, Olive, so why don't we start with my question? What the hell are you doing here?" he shouted.

"I work here," Olive lied, for the sake of not having to explain herself. "I told you I was going to find a job, did I not? How did you get in here, anyway? The bar is closed for the owner's mother's birthday."

"Bullshit, Olive! It's past midnight, and he's still here with you. Who is he?" Adam loomed over Jepson, who was still lying motionless on the floor.

"Don't touch him, Adam!"

"'Don't touch him?' Oh, I'm pretty sure I'm going to *kill* your little beau here."

"Adam, no—!" She managed to force a calm, assertive tone. "It's not like that. *He's* not like that."

"Don't feed me your lies, witch! We're going home. You'll be staying in the house from now on, do you hear? Your job here is done. You are *my* wife!"

"I won't let you tell me what to do, Adam! I can make my own decisions." Olive stood tall and confident in front of the booth, holding her ground.

Adam snorted, a rumble beginning to creep from the back of his throat. He approached Olive, bearing a menacing grimace. "You are allowed to do what I tell you you're allowed to do, and I'm telling you that we're going home!"

"I'm not going home with you, Adam!" Her voice grew higher and began to break. "I know what you did to those chickens, and I know what you did to my family's cow."

"*Your* family? Olive, those people aren't your family anymore! I ran into my father tonight. He was closing up his woodshop for the night. His *woodshop!* My father, the king, is a *wood smith!* And what's worse—he has no idea who I am! The man was terrified of me! He just looked at me like I was a hideous animal! I begged him to remember me. I needed *my father* to know who I am, but he just backed away and told me he didn't have a son, and then ran as fast as he could to get away!"

"I'm so sorry, dear." Olive teared up a bit watching her husband in pain. "I know it's heartbreaking, and I don't know what to tell you except that I know it's all going to be okay. It's already getting better, if you let me explain. We just have to keep moving forward—"

"We are in Hell, Olive! Have you not figured this out yet?" Adam screamed. "We died in that storm and we got sent to Hell. That cow didn't belong to your family. It belonged to impostors. They are not people. They are creatures of Hell who took the form of your family. There is no moving forward. There's nothing we can do to fix this."

"But that's not true!" Olive was crying now. "Just please, let me take you along with me tomorrow. I can show you how things are. It's not all bad."

"Everyone hates me! Nobody wants to look at me! Why would I want to go out during the day?"

"I don't look well either, dear. ~~I know~~. And yes, people stop and stare, and they say things that can be hurtful, but Adam, you have no control over what you look like right now. What you do have control over is your *behavior*. Adam, you've been violent to me, and I suspect you have to others, too. You've been cruel, and you've secluded yourself, ~~too,~~ which is only making things worse. Have you even tried to go out during the day? Talking with people might help, even if they're scared at first. Please come with me tomorrow."

"I don't want to go with you! I won't be a third wheel in your stupid little romance. I am your husband, and you're going home with me!" He snarled and reached for Olive's shoulder with his massive furry hand. She tried again to regain the calm assertiveness she'd had before, but she crumbled with sadness and fear instead as she looked into Adam's beady black eyes.

A loud crash sounded behind Adam. Confusion illuminated his beady stare. He turned to find Jepson standing on the bar top across the room with an empty bottle in each hand.

"Run, Basketcase! I don't want to hurt you, too." Jepson was on his toes, ready for a fight.

"Jepson, no! You don't understand. Please don't hurt him!"

Adam pulled Olive by her hips and slumped her over his shoulders. He headed for the door, but Jepson threw two more bottles at his feet. The bottles shattered, spewing shards of glass between Adam's toes. Adam yelped in pain and turned back towards Jepson with rage in his eyes, dropping Olive on the hard wooden floor to free his hands. Olive tucked herself into a ball and rolled underneath a booth near the door for safety.

"You asshole!" Adam shouted at Jepson. He picked up one of the smaller tables and threw it at the bar top.

Jepson ducked behind the bar, emerging a moment later holding a clear glass bottle filled with dark liquor, which he held above his head before chucking it at Adam.

The bottle spun several times as it flew, then shattered at Adam's feet. The black whiskey from inside the bottle sizzled as it settled into Adam's fresh wounds. Jepson held his fists against his hips and snubbed his nose as he watched the beast of a man fall over onto the floor, whining in pain.

A moment later, though, it was clear that Adam's anguish was for show. He sprang up again, grimacing with a wheezy chuckle. "That's all you got, pansy?" he scoffed. "I can fight wussy-style, too."

Adam sauntered over to the cake on the table. He made a fist and punched the table a few feet from where the cake stood, untouched.

"Don't you touch that cake, Beast. I *will* kill you." Jepson and Adam locked glares.

Adam scooped a fistful of cake right off the top and then licked it off his hand. "Nothing special," he said, swallowing.

Both Olive and Jepson cringed. Cakes from Grimm's Bakery were always fantastic.

Adam said nothing as he approached the bar again. He lowered himself onto all fours in an animalistic pre-pounce. "You may be large, pretty boy, but I know you ain't gonna hurt me. You don't even know how."

Jepson kept his glare focused on Adam and mirrored the animal-like poise from his place on top of the bar. "Who are you, Beast?"

Adam cackled and licked his lips, but before he could open his mouth to answer, Olive pulled herself from underneath the booth to stand behind him. "He's my husband!" she shouted. "Don't hurt him."

Both men turned to look at her.

"He's not a beast," she said. "He's not a bad person, but he's become sad in a way I can't even begin to explain. He needs me now more than ever."

Neither man said a word, but continued to stare at her.

"Let's go, Adam. I'd like to go home with you now." She spoke in a soft tone and held out her hand.

Adam made a slow, hesitant move in her direction, and Olive realized how afraid he looked. She gazed at him with love but kept an eye on Jepson, who made a quick jerking motion atop the bar.

"Stay where you are!" Olive pointed a finger at him and stared him straight in the eyes. "Don't you follow us, either. Let's go, Adam."

Olive took Adam's hand and led him towards the door of the bar.

"Wait! Basketca—"

"It's *Olive!*" She shot a deep, angry look in Jepson's direction. "My name is Olive Grimm."

CHAPTER 14
The Clock, the Candlestick & the Wall

"Just tell me who he is, for real. Don't you bullshit me." Adam sat cross-legged on the floor across from Olive in the sitting room of their home.

"Can you please not bring up cow shit, after what you did?" Olive snapped.

It was still very dark, but Olive was wide awake after having slept so long at the bar. She didn't feel tired, sad, or even angry. As much as she'd tried to be supportive and compassionate towards Adam after they'd returned home, she was numb inside.

"Just tell me who he is."

"He's a friend. He was kind to me. I don't know why, but he was. Just a friend, nothing more." Her tone was lifeless.

"You're sleeping with him, aren't you?"

"No, Adam. I'm not."

"Olive, you were both sleeping! In the same room."

"He was on the floor. I was not. You saw that."

"Why didn't you just come home to sleep?"

Olive took a deep breath and tried to align her thoughts. "Adam, I know what you did to those chickens."

"Don't change the goddamn subject!" he yelled.

He stood and paced the room twice before snatching an empty vase from a side table. He threw it past Olive and against the wall behind her. The vase shattered, and a small piece of porcelain flew into Olive's eye.

"Augh—ow! What was that for?" She rubbed her eye with dirty fingers as she tried to remove the piece of porcelain. Her mind flashed back to the day after the storm, when Adam had thrown the piece of stained glass at her.

"I told you how I got those eggs! Don't accuse me of something I didn't do. We're talking about *him* now, so don't turn this around on me. I want you to tell me everything, and then I'm going to kill him."

"Adam, you are all over the place. There's nothing more to tell you about Jepson. You were too depressed to leave the house, and I needed a friend. Jepson found me and helped me and now he and I are friends. He is not my lover and he never will be. He's not like that. He doesn't even—never mind."

"He's your friend now, but he was your boss an hour ago. How can I trust anything you say if your story keeps changing?" Adam picked up a candlestick and threw it so it just missed Olive and hit an end table behind her.

"Adam, stop! Why are you trying to hurt me?" She was still sitting on the floor, hoping her non-threatening position would help to calm Adam.

"Oh, poor you. Why am I hurting you? I'm not even hurting you that bad. Why are you doing this to *me?*"

"What am I doing to you, Adam? Please, tell me what I can do to make you happy!"

"Nothing! You're doing nothing to me, Olive! That's the fucking problem! You're gone all day, and you ignore me. I want you to stay and keep me company while I'm going through all this."

"But you won't *go* with *me!* I'm gone all day because you lay in your drawing room and cry all day, and I *will not* do that to myself! Also, we're *both* going through this together! Quit acting like you're the only victim here. All of this affects us both."

He approached her, crouching down to where she sat, bringing his face close to hers in a menacing way. "You have been a commoner your whole life. All of this is normal for you. But I lost my goddamn kingdom! Did you think about that?"

"None of those things mean anything, Your goddamn Majesty, Prince Adam of Sidney!" Olive stood, shaking her head in disgust as she backed away from him. "You lost your crown? Yeah, well, I lost my pet cow! Want to tell me more about your hand in that, Your Highness?"

Olive had just finished the last word in the sentence when Adam picked up a mantlepiece clock and threw it across the room at her. The face of the clock bashed into her nose, shooting cold pain through her sinuses. She yelped as she fell to the floor again. With blood dripping from her nose, she held her hand over her face and brought herself forward so that she was stabilized on her free hand and ~~both~~ knees. Just as a large droplet of blood fell to the hardwood floor beneath her, a lock of soft, curly hair slipped from her right temple.

It dangled in front of her eyes. Olive paused, looking at the curl and smiling through her bloodstained fingers. It was on the same side of her head as the curl in the back. She couldn't help but let out a happy squeal, which could not have clashed more with the grim air of the sitting room. She let all her anger and sadness from the night wash away for a moment as she caressed the soft, flowing locks that graced the right half of her head.

"Things are getting better, Adam. Whatever caused this, it isn't permanent. I can show you."

Adam wasn't looking at her anymore. He had his back to her and was glowering out the window.

"Last night when I came home," she started, "you had cleaned yourself. You looked nice. We made love. Couldn't you feel things changing?"

"You are so full of shit." He spun back around with wild abruptness, causing Olive to flinch. "I fucked you because it was the only thing that would make me feel like a man again."

"Exactly! You felt like a *man* again, instead of like a—"

"A what? Say it! A bear? A werewolf? What the hell am I, Olive?" His voice broke into sobs.

"Things are changing, dear. You can say what you want, but I know you feel it, too. Haven't you noticed anything different about me? How could you miss it?" She ran her fingers through the dark, smooth, untangled half of her hair.

Adam cocked his head and beamed as he reached for the piece of Olive's hair. For a moment, he looked intrigued. She pulled away from him as he drew closer to her, although she continued to hold out a curl for him to see.

He stared for a long moment before speaking. "How did you do this?"

"I've been trying to tell you, dear. I go out into the town, and I talk with people. I've made friends, and I've tried to make the most of our bad situation. I've been making an effort to be good to people no matter how angry I feel. It hasn't been easy, though. The anger I've been feeling is stronger than anything I've ever felt before. It's when I resist it, though, that I feel things changing."

He looked back at her with knowing eyes. "So, you feel it, too?"

"Yes! Yes, I do!" A rush of relief cooled over her, and she reached up to place her hands on his shoulders. "Oh Adam, isn't it awful? We don't have to feel that way anymore. It isn't you that wants to do those things. It is, but it's complicated. I can teach you! I was able to—"

He pulled away from her, looking insulted. "What are you saying? That power is what makes me feel strong, like a hunter in my natural state. It's like a game. I don't want that to go away."

"Adam, no! It's just not right. Please listen to me." Her words were hurried as she tried to explain. "That power you're feeling doesn't belong to you. There are things—creatures—that are using us to do terrible things, but you don't have to do what they say. You can turn it right back against them."

He glowered at her. "You are *insane!* Are you listening to yourself? You sound like a goddamn basket case!"

She paused and rolled her eyes. "What does that word even mean? Do you realize that what I'm saying isn't any more bizarre than everything we've been through already? We both know that everything we've witnessed these last few days is impossible, correct? And yet, when I try and tell you there's something inside your head controlling you, you tell me *I'm* crazy? Adam, *all of this* is crazy, and none of it makes sense, but I can show you how to overpower it."

"I don't *want* to overpower it!" Adam shouted. "Stop this now! You're making a fool of yourself."

"Dear, you want things to change back, do you not? Overpowering this might be the only way to change it. Look at my *hair*, Adam! Clearly, I know something you don't. Please listen. I can help!"

"Oh, fuck your hair! It probably just means your shitlocks on the other side are even worse now."

"Why are you being so mean? This isn't like you! You were a good man before, Adam!"

Adam gruffed. "I was a good man when my life was going the way it was supposed to go. Now I'm not even sure if there's any man left inside me to be a good one. I'm just angry, *all* the time!"

"Please don't be this way," Olive sobbed. "Of course you're still a man! I know things are horrible and very strange right now, but being cruel is not the solution. The reason you're talking down to me and calling me all these names is because you're too sad to listen to what I have to say. Adam, please, I'm angry, too, but I promise I can help you. I *want* to help you."

"The only help I need is to get rid of you." He glowered at her. "You're a witch, and you always have been. I knew it all along, and I ignored it. Everyone knows your family is wicked."

"What? Where is all of this coming from? One minute you tell me I'm not around enough, and the next you say you're getting rid of me? You're not making any sense!" Olive's voice was quick and frantic. "And where did you hear those things about my family? I've never heard a soul say anything like that."

"*Everyone* says that!" he shouted.

"Who, then? Are you making up stories to get a rise out of me?" Olive crossed her arms and walked across the sitting room towards him.

"It doesn't matter anymore. They're gone." Adam paced back and forth along the wall near the window.

"No, they're not! My brother Lionel—"

"Doesn't remember you?" Adam suggested.

"No, but I think he's starting to." Her heart sank a bit.

Adam stopped pacing. His dark expression met with Olive's wide eyes. "Everything is fucked," he hammered. "If you're so convinced that you know how to make everything better, then you're either stupid, or—"

"Or what?" Olive asked.

"Or you're the one who made it this way." He threw his arms up in an accusatory manner.

"Adam, stop with that! Listen to me!" Olive had heard enough. She'd grown impatient with him not listening to reason and saying hurtful things. She was beginning to lose her temper. "Why are you being so terrible to me! I hate this, please just listen to me!"

Through her swirl of panic, Olive felt disoriented and winded as something large smashed against her back. Pain shot up her spine and neck and into the back of her head. Her neck spasmed as she sat up and realized the wall was behind her. She felt sick, realizing what had just happened.

"You threw me against the wall, Adam! Why?" she screeched. "Why are you doing this? Why are you hurting me?"

"It was an accident. You should have just let me be." Adam was solemn and quiet now, as if his actions had calmed him. He stood with his back to her again, looking out the window into the blackness outside.

"Let you be. Stay with you. I'm ignoring you. I'm pestering you. Which one is it, you spoiled-rotten piece of shit?!"

He turned to her, his eyes dark and narrowed. Olive's nerves lit up with fear and fury, her ears hissing.

"Oh, shut up, you scaly old hag!" She responded to the hissing sound, forcing positive thoughts to the front of her mind. She cupped her hands over her ears and massaged her aching temples, making sure to keep her eyes closed as she envisioned a field of colorful daisies. The hissing silenced almost right away, which was much quicker than Olive had anticipated.

Olive kept her eyes closed and her head bent. The room remained warm, and she could see only darkness through her eyelids.

She snickered with an air of triumph. "I knew you little twits would do what I told you to do."

She could hear Adam grunting and stomping across the room towards her.

"Don't you hurt me again, Adam. Those words were not meant for you." Her voice was firm and confident.

His breath quickened with anxiety. "You crazy bitch! Who else would you be talking to? The voices inside your head?"

She opened her eyes and looked up at him, smirking. "My inner demons, Adam? Yes, I was talking to the creatures inside my head, and it's helping. Please let me show you how to do it."

"Witch!" he shouted, backing away from her and almost tripping over the candlestick he'd thrown earlier. He grabbed it instead and hurled it towards the window where he'd been pacing. It hit the windowsill, dropping back to the floor. "I *had* to marry a Grimm!" he wailed at the ceiling. "I welcomed a *Grimm* into the royal family! How could I have been so stupid?"

He chased down the candlestick before throwing it once more, this time in Olive's direction. She was caught off-guard by the quick throw, and the candlestick hit her on the side of her forehead. The hard metal corner gouged the thin skin on her upper eyebrow and temple, drawing blood that ran down her cheek and onto the torn, withered shoulder of her dress.

"Adam, this is enough! I've tried to help, but you don't want my help. You only want my pity, and I can't give you that. We're in this together, and we can get out of this together."

"You want to know how you can help me?" His crouched down, his dark eyes meeting hers. "Stop pretending like everything is just fine and dandy. I want to hear you say that we're in Hell. I want you to look me in the eye and tell me how sorry you are for what you've done. I've lost my fortune, my royal status, and my family. You can at least pretend to feel sorry for me."

"I do feel sorry for you, Adam. I feel sorry for *us*, but I already told you that I won't pity you. I won't even pity myself. That's not how I do things."

He lunged at her then, and she covered her face with her arms. He grabbed her around the waist instead and lifted her above his head. She kicked her legs and stiffened her abdomen in an attempt to make him drop her, but he slung her over his shoulder and held onto both of her legs. The hold made it difficult to move anything except her arms, and even then, the angle didn't help her situation at all.

Adam stalked from the sitting room back towards the staircase, continuing to hold Olive in a stiff and uncomfortable position.

"Adam! Put me down! Where are you taking me?" she screamed.

"You don't know this house very well, do you?" he said with amusement.

"Put me down, Adam! Put me down!" She screeched and flailed as much as she could, but he held onto her tight.

As they ascended the staircase, a step creaked, sending a small plank of wood to the floor below.

"Stupid piece of shit house!" he howled, shaking the walls around them.

Olive succumbed to the lump that had been growing in her throat. Silent tears poured down her cheeks, and a moment later Adam dropped her onto a cold wooden floor in a dark room. She let herself fall onto her side and curled her legs up against her stomach, attempting to cover as much of her body as she could with her skirt. She said nothing as Adam turned his back to her and walked back towards the door.

"Stay here and think about what you've done," he growled.

He slammed the door behind him as he left, causing the walls and floor to shake and groan. Olive heard the click of a lock behind him as she lay quiet and still amid a growing puddle of her own tears.

CHAPTER 15
Imprisonment
Day Five

We fell in love. He loved me so.
We got married and moved out here on our own.
But then we changed. I wish I knew
how we can fix this even though I think I'm through.

Olive sat in an oblong square of light on the floor several hours later, strumming a wooden mandolin. The guest room where Adam had left her was smaller than their bedroom, with two shuttered windows on the far wall that let in a fair amount of light around the edges. She had attempted to open the shutters to climb out or call for help, but the thick wooden frames had either been jammed shut or fastened closed from the outside.

She'd found the mandolin on the wall next to the bed, along with several other stringed instruments. All of which were warped and dirty with age, and missing at least one string. All except for the mandolin.

Olive had played mandolin from a young age but had abandoned the hobby since meeting Adam. Like the rest of the house, the mandolin was in rough shape. Its rusted strings and musty wood came together to produce a twangy, muddy sound. She finger-picked a silly children's song she hadn't thought about in years; her heart and mind flooded with memories of sitting in the grass behind her family's bakery, putting melodies to nursery rhymes.

Adam had been quiet since leaving her in the room. She wondered when he was planning to return, but at the same time, she enjoyed the privacy and solitude. Her back and neck still ached from Adam throwing her around, but she felt best unbothered. For the first time since the night of the supermoon, she let go of her urge to move forward. She surrendered to the quiet sanctity.

Beyond the room, there was a world just as real and warped and chaotic as it always had been. Though different, the Land of Sidney was no more or less evil than it had been before. The only thing worse was the present state of Adam and Olive's luck: a series of unfortunate events that Olive was still trying to convince herself were a temporary misadventure to overcome.

He was so sweet, but now he's sad.
He thinks I did this, and I know that makes him mad.
Oh, how he's changed. How I have, too.
It's just not fair—I wish I knew what to do.

She strummed along to her song as she dreamt up another verse. She repeated the lyrics to herself over and over and realized how ordinary they sounded. Though she and Adam's current situation was far from acceptable or believable, the narrative she'd written sounded almost identical to issues she'd overheard her parents and other couples argue over time and time again.

She wondered if what was happening to her and Adam had ever happened to anyone else. She considered the idea that other families who'd been down on their luck, or people who'd lost their minds, were or had done so because of similar unexplainable experiences. The idea soothed her. She wished she had a piece of paper and a pen so she could write a short story about it.

Thunder rolled outside, shaking the wooden floor where she sat. The patter of raindrops started up and intensified within minutes. A cool breeze filtered through the cracks around the shuttered window, hitting her shoulders and sending a chill up her arms and spine. Olive stood, shivering. She placed the mandolin at the foot of the small bed, then climbed under the warm comforter.

The bedding in the room smelled different than the sheets and blankets in her and Adam's room. Everything had a cleaner, milkier scent here, similar to the dress she'd picked from her closet that morning. She laid her head on the pillow and pulled the blanket up over her shoulders, making sure to leave her ears uncovered so she could hear and enjoy the storm outside. She fell into a comfortable sleep for the first time in days as the rain soothed her bruised muscles and soul.

Olive awoke sometime later, attempting to ignore the loud pounding from outside the bedroom door. The room was cold, but she was still warm and comfortable beneath the covers.

"Olive! I'm hungry!" Adam yelled from behind the door, continuing to pound on it.

She covered her head with the blankets and groaned.

"It's locked, Adam! You have to unlock it for me if you want to come in." She rolled her eyes and buried herself further underneath the bedding.

She heard Adam turn the door handle before heading back down the hallway.

"What? Aren't you coming in?" Confused and bewildered by her husband's naivety, she turned and faced the window again to distract herself. The storm was loud and chaotic, but her eyes had adjusted to the dark enough so that she could see tiny droplets of water seeping in around the shutters.

She heard Adam again. He fumbled with a key outside the bedroom door, dropping it several times before turning the lock with success. He was sopping wet and smelled like a damp animal.

"Were you outside?" she asked.

"No."

"That's a lie." She huffed.

"Well, what do you want me to tell you?"

"The truth, Adam. I want you to be honest with me."

He threw his arms up. "Alright, I went outside."

"It's daytime still, is it not?" she asked.

"What does that matter?" His voice was high and defensive.

"You don't go out during the day." Her voice held a contemptuous tone.

He grunted. "It's dark enough from the storm."

"So, I'm curious—" she sat up, keeping the blanket pulled around her "—is it the light that keeps you in, or the idea that people will see you? What'll happen if you try and leave with me during the day? We don't have to go into town, but I want to get you outside at least when the weather clears up. I think it'll be good for you."

The yellow rim around his dark eyes flashed in her direction. Even in the dark room, she could see the pain in his gaze.

"I don't know what'll happen, alright?" he whispered. "It just hurts to think about."

"Adam." She forced a soft tone. "I want you to try. Why don't you and I go outside after it stops raining? The smell of the rain and earth will be like medicine for your soul. I don't think it'll hurt you the way you think it will."

"I'm depressed, okay, Olive? I don't want to be uncomfortable as well."

"Did you not hear anything I just said?" She was losing patience again. "Comfortable? Adam, you threw me against a wall this morning! You threw a candlestick and a clock at me, and then locked me in a room! Fuck your comfort. What about mine?"

"I told you that was an accident!" he shouted, snatching a decorative teapot from an end table by the door and throwing it at Olive.

She ducked, the teapot to shattering against the headboard behind her. The continual, unending violent streak was becoming too much for her to handle. Her heart sank, her muscles went slack, and she covered her face with her hands. She was too anxious to form a logical thought that would allow her to move from her place on the bed.

"These things you're doing, Adam—are not accidents! You are hurting me on purpose." Olive said between her teeth.

"I do not *want* to hurt you!" he shouted. "You just need to stop acting like you're better than me. It's your choice. If you stop, I'll stop."

Olive wrapped the blankets around her body in a way that helped her to feel secure, even if it was only in a mental way. She moved to her knees on the bed and tilted in Adam's direction. "Adam, are you trying to tell me *your* behavior is *my* fault?"

"Yes! You won't listen to me. You won't be there for me. You've been kicking me when I'm down this whole time! I don't want to hurt you, Olive, but when you disrespect me like this, it's *going* to happen. I'm going to keep hurting you as long as you keep acting this way. You act like you know so much, but you don't know anything about anything! If you want me to stop hurting you, you need to stop all of this."

"Stop what, Adam? What have I done to deserve your violent behavior towards me?"

"This! This whole thing you're doing: sneaking around with other men, talking to me like I'm a child, telling me I need to do things I don't want to do."

"We *all* have to do things we don't want to do, you spoiled piece of royal shit!"

Thunder cracked through the air and a bolt of lightning from outside lit up the room for a split second. Adam gave a deep roar, answered the sound. He grabbed the small mandolin from the foot of the bed where Olive had left it and held it by the neck high above his head. He whipped the mandolin in midair, making Olive flinch, which made Adam laugh. He walked around the room, pretending to bat it at each of the walls, but stopped short and recoiled each time.

"Adam, what the fuck? That's not funny. You have no reason to break that." She climbed out from underneath the covers and got tangled in the sheets as she scrambled out of the bed. Her knee and hip thudded against the hard floor as she fell.

"Ow! God dammit!" She grabbed the bedpost to steady herself and found that Adam was standing just inches in front of her, edging her against the side of the bed and blocking her from standing.

"Adam, please move so I can get up," she ordered him.

"Are you going to join me for dinner without acting like a bitch?" He turned his nose up at her, even though she was still kneeling, and he was already looming over her.

"I'm not hungry," she lied.

"Then you'll stay in here until you're ready to eat, and then I'll let you come downstairs and make us some food."

"I'm not cooking for you anymore, Adam."

"You're my wife, Olive! You'll do what I tell you to do!"

"Husbands don't hurt their wives." She shook her head, frowning. "I'm done helping you until you can see that."

"I don't hurt you that bad! You know that. I don't beat you. I could if I wanted to, but I don't because I don't *want* to hurt you. It's not fair to punish me because of that, so can you just please come downstairs and help me a little?" His words were shaky and desperate.

"No." She continued shaking her head at him. "Not today, I won't."

Adam growled again, and the walls shook around them. Without moving from his place in front of her, he swung the mandolin again, this time against the bedpost above her head. The body of the mandolin broke apart from the neck, the pieces held together by splintered wood and metal strings. Olive cringed and whimpered, as if she had watched the beheading of a close friend.

"Didn't you go into town already?" she asked between sobs. She was still kneeling at his waist, trapped between the bed and Adam's large, solid body.

"I went into the woods," he answered.

She pursed her lips together, knowing she shouldn't provoke him from her vulnerable position, but as the rage within her grew, her strength did as well. The familiar hissing sounds started up inside her ears, but this time it was different. Figments of the song she had written resonated in her memory and mixed with the jaunty tunes Jepson had played. The music, even the sad parts, helped Olive to feel happy and bright. The hissing sound continued at a steady pace, though instead of growing louder as it had in the past, the sounds blended and harmonized together like a symphonic fairytale.

Half of Olive's soul felt strong and confident then, while the other half felt angrier than she'd ever been before. As she looked up at Adam from where she knelt pinned against the side of the bed, the feelings danced together, giving her permission to do what she had to do to defend herself.

She cocked her head and looked up at Adam, gritting her teeth as she spoke. "If you were just in the woods, then you don't even need me, do you? You've had your dinner already."

His bloodshot eyes widened as he looked down at her. He held the mandolin up over his head again, ready to swing. His slight change in position gave Olive just enough space so that she could fold herself in half, bringing her chest to the floor underneath the bed. She used her arms to push herself backwards on her stomach until she slid out the other side of the bed, steadying herself but staying low to the floor. Adam spotted her and dove around the footboard, but Olive had already leapt onto the bed, somersaulting over the top and tumbling off the other side so that she was very close to the door.

She reached for the doorknob, a single finger touching the cold metal before she could feel the sharp wooden shards of the mandolin scratch the back of her neck. The metal ends of broken strings pierced her scalp and drew blood down her shoulders and back. She gasped with pain and fear, but what she feared was her own fate and the harm she was facing. She wasn't afraid of Adam any longer, she decided.

It was at that moment she was able to see that it had always been cowardice that had guided Adam's cruelty. The hissing sounds danced with the melodies inside her head, growing louder and more intense and reminding her that it was time to do whatever had to be done to ensure her own safety and well-being.

"*Out!*" she screamed with power that resonated off the walls and the floor, the blood from her shoulders collecting down the front of her dress. "Get out of my room!"

"Your room?" He chuckled in a demeaning way, still holding the fragments of the mandolin. "You know damn well that this is *my* house, right?"

"Get out, Adam. *Get out* of my room—*now.*" Her voice boomed, and the choir of encouragement bounced triumphantly in her ears. "*Out—out—OUT!*"

A howl escaped her throat on the last word, unlike any sound she had ever been able to make before. It echoed through their home and caused the walls to vibrate and hiss around them like an epic symphony. Hundreds of bolts of silent lightning flashed outside the shuttered window, creating an almost steady stream of light inside the room. Olive was able to see into every corner of the room for the first time. The details in the moldings on the wall and the designs in the bedspread danced in the flickering light.

She looked down at Adam, who was now hunched near the floor and shivering. Though the room was brighter for her now, she could tell by the look of Adam's pupils that he was still peering into darkness.

The hissing sounds, which continued inside her ears and throughout the air in the room, were soon accompanied by loud popping and squealing. The sound crackled and whistled like a campfire doused with cold water. All the pressure and pain that had been building inside her temples and between her ears cracked and broke apart, draining from her chest and legs and creating a pool of light on the floor beneath her. A feeling of sanctity washed over her, and her thoughts were clear and calm.

Olive felt powerful, but in a different way than before. This new power was neither malicious nor harmful. It was a colorful and bright energy, one that danced with the lightning and harmonized with the vibrations in the walls. She could no longer see into Adam's soul, nor did she want to hurt him. The energy was there for her protection.

The thunder and lightning mellowed and subsided. The room was dark and still again, with nothing but the soft pink haze of the sunset seeping through the cracks in the shutters.

"Please leave now, Adam. I want to be alone," she said.

Adam scrambled to his feet, his eyes wide with fear. "You—are crazy!" He pointed at her with a shaky index finger, approaching with caution.

"Please let me be," she demanded.

"You—" he continued to point at her—"I knew you were a witch."

"Adam, I won't discuss this with you any longer."

"You're out of here tomorrow. Get out of my life. You are not my wife anymore. I'm done with you, witch!"

Olive said nothing as she watched Adam scramble out the door and slam it behind him. She exhaled, releasing one last cathartic hiss and squeal into the air as exhaustion set in again. She stumbled forward, her eyes rolling back inside her head and she fell sideways onto the bed.

CHAPTER 16
Shine & Grime
Day Six

The first thing Olive noticed when she opened her eyes were the shutters. They were wide open, allowing sunlight and fresh, crisp air to pour into the little bedroom. Chirping birds flew past the window, and specks of snow floated from the tall evergreen trees outside.

She smiled and laughed, her heart fluttering with excitement. Her skin, hair and clothing felt fresh, clean, and soft. The air outside was crisp and happy, and even the bedding underneath her smelled freshly laundered, complete with hints of lavender and cardamom. The wooden molding on the walls had been dusted and polished, and the wood floors underneath her gleamed with newness.

Frantic with happiness, Olive got out of bed, exploring the freshness of the room and of herself. She examined all sides of her head with her hands to find that all four matted locks had turned back into her usual curls. The room had no closet: only a large armoire. Behind each of the double doors of the armoire was a mirror, between which hung a simple blue dress and a small pair of lace-up boots. She used the mirrors to check that her face and hair had returned to their normal, healthy colors, and then dressed in the comfortable outfit. Finally, she tore a strip from the dress she'd worn the day before and used it to tie back half of her hair.

She paced the room, the excitement of her discoveries consuming her. The day before, she had almost convinced herself that she wasn't bothered by the unexplainable events, but now that everything was shifting back into place, she felt euphoric. She ran to the open window and stuck her head as far out as she could without falling. "Hello!" she called out, to no one in particular. "Bonjour! Hello! Hello! Hello!"

She twirled around the room and ran to the door, turning the doorknob less than an inch before it fell off the door and onto the floor with a metallic clank. The door creaked open to reveal a dark and dingy hallway.

Olive's breathing slowed. She looked back and forth between the beautiful room and the grimy hallway that still smelled of mold. With a heavy heart and a disappointed sigh, she held her breath as she entered the hall and took off towards the stairs, which were in worse shape than they ever had been. She felt certain she'd fall through even if she was careful.

Gripping the thick wooden handrail, she shook it to test its strength. The railing moved back and forth, but it stayed solid and whole. She took another deep breath and held it to steady herself before placing her legs around the handrail as if she were sitting on a horse, sliding down the railing and dismounting in the dining room at the bottom.

A cracking noise resonated from the top of the stairs. The railing swayed back and forth before breaking free from the upstairs wall and falling inward, smashing through what was left of the broken steps. A slab of floorboard hung where the top step had been torn from it, causing the walls around Olive to deliver an agonizing creak. They whined in the wind, warning her to leave.

"Adam!" she called. "Adam! Please, where are you?"

She covered her head with both hands and started towards the drawing room in search of him. He had been cruel to her, but she was determined to help him make it safely out of the house. And, although she had her doubts, she also hoped he'd woken up in as good shape as she had.

The creaking noises followed Olive through the sitting room and to the doorway towards the hallway that led to Adam's drawing room. She touched the wooden molding around the doorframe, which she could feel vibrating and buzzing, followed by a sudden intense crack from the ceiling above it. She pulled her arm back just as the doorframe fell in on itself, leaving the path to the long hallway a dangerous pile of splintered wood.

The house moaned and warned more and more. Cracks appeared along the ceiling above Olive's head, growing longer and following her as she made her way through the dining room and out the front door.

"Adam!" she called from the front yard. "*Adam!*"

She swept the tears from her eyes and stumbled towards the Sidney commons, which were calm and cheery in comparison. The air was chilly but refreshing, and the townspeople wore smiles at the novelty of donning knitted hats and scarves for the first time in months. The positive energy of the common grounds soothed Olive's nerves. She forced a smile and took a deep breath as she walked at a steady pace into town. Her mind still raced with anxiety knowing that Adam was trapped inside the imploding house, but she continued telling herself that panicking would only make things worse.

CHAPTER 17
Sustenance & Support

Olive headed towards JB's Tavern, where she planned to apologize for Adam's behavior. She decided she would remain confident and stand her ground about needing Jepson's help to save Adam.

"Olive!" a man's voice shouted far behind her.

Olive shivered and walked away from the voice. Her face was hot, her feet felt numb, and her fingers were icy. Someone behind her yanked her arm.

"Stop hurting me!" she screeched.

Jepson stared back at Olive, wide-eyed and pink-cheeked in the crisp weather. Olive's heartbeat steadied as her fear was replaced by embarrassment.

"It's you." She went pale and looked at her feet, forgetting everything she'd planned to tell him.

Jepson's stare didn't waver. "You look terrible, Olive. Are you ok?"

"I don't look terrible," she snapped. "I'm wearing a clean dress, and—and my hair is tied back, and it's not even tangled anymore, look! I woke up today, and everything is just different. It's like right before I met you, there was a storm, and somehow my entire life and everything I ever knew about Sidney changed. Well, it's getting better. I mean, I woke up today, and the room I was sleeping in was just beautiful. And yesterday, I played mandolin and wrote a song and—I think I made lightning, too!"

"Basketcase! Calm down. Your hair and dress are not the problems. You look pale and tired. Do you need some food? When was the last time you ate?"

Olive had been too excited that morning to think about food or water, but as soon as Jepson asked, she realized that she had not eaten or drunk anything since two nights earlier, when Adam had locked her in the room. In her sudden state of delirium and hunger, Jepson's mention of food was all she could think about.

"I'm thirsty, yes." She nodded. "Hungry, too."

Jepson nodded, offering her the flask he had clipped to his belt. "It's tea," he said, "no booze. It's cold now, though, so drink it fast if you want."

She gulped down the remainder of the tea from the flask, feeling a bit dizzy as she handed it back to Jepson. "Food. More tea, please. Chilled, like that."

Jepson nodded, placing a supportive arm around her as he led her inside a nearby building. He pulled out a chair for her at a small table near a crackling fireplace. She sat down without saying a word, and he sat across from her.

"Two bowls of meatball soup as soon as possible, please," she heard him say to someone nearby. "And if you have a pot of tea that's gotten cold, we'd love that, too."

Olive groaned, folding her arms on the table and resting her head in the crook of her elbow.

"Don't fall asleep yet, Basketcase." Jepson pushed a cup of cold tea across the table to her. "Food first, then you can sleep."

She took a small sip before speaking. "I need to talk to you. I know I do—did—but can't even 'member of what." Her words came out strange and staggered and confusing.

"Two bowls of meatball soup?" A familiar voice pulled Olive back to reality.

She turned her head towards the voice and recognized the man's face. The man looked back at her with a plastery smile and forced friendly demeanor that she knew he reserved for his customers. The man smiled with his eyes when he was happy for real, and he was always funnier and wittier around people he knew and loved.

"We've met before, have we not, dear?" the man asked.

"Yes, Papa, we have," she answered.

The man's face twisted in confusion then, and he looked to Jepson for an explanation.

"Olive here is, uh, an old friend of Lionel's," Jepson jumped in. "Might have played at your house when she was a kid. Girl's been going through a rough patch and acts a bit goofy sometimes."

Olive took a large spoonful of her soup and savored the familiar, nostalgic flavor.

"Well, that's very kind of you to take care of her, Jepson, but I recognize your friend here from a time that's much more recent. Dear, didn't you used to work in our store down the road? Grimm's Bakery, do you know of it?"

"Yes, sir," she answered through a mouthful of soup, sputtering some onto the tablecloth. "I used to manage that bakery."

The man looked at her again, cocking his head in a quizzical fashion. "Not likely, dear. That's a job we leave to family."

"Okay, Basketcase, it's time to finish your soup," Jepson said hurriedly, "and we'll find you someplace to take a nap."

"Can't you see I'm talking with someone?" she whined.

"It's not kind to call the girl a basket-case if she's indeed not right, Jepson," the man added.

"I'm right here, Papa!" She shot the man a look. "I can hear you talking about me."

"Okay, Olive. We're leaving," Jepson said, standing and tugging Olive's elbow towards the door.

"I want to finish my soup!" she shouted.

"Basketcase, we are going *now!*" His look was serious and still.

She shoveled in a few more mouthfuls of soup before letting Jepson lead her out the front door of the restaurant.

"It says Grimm's Eatery on the front of this building," Olive started. "But this isn't where we had it before! Everything is still different. It didn't work."

"What were you doing, Basketcase?" Jepson shouted after walking a little ways down the road. "I can't just let you embarrass me like that! You really are a basket case, aren't you?"

"It didn't work," she whined. "I thought everything was back to normal, but it's not. I thought I fixed it. I even made lightning, and I could see in the dark and everything, but it's still all fucked up!"

"Olive, you need to stop all of this!" He paused, turning to shake her shoulders. He held onto her cheeks to keep her still while he pulled down on her bottom eyelids, inspecting each eye. "Are you ill? Did he do something to you, your husband? Did he drug or poison you?"

"Oh, no! Adam!" she shrieked, feeling a mix of contempt, fear and responsibility saying his name aloud. "How could I have forgotten? Jepson, Adam needs your help. The house, it's falling apart! Oh no, it's probably too late now! What is wrong with me? We have to go find him!"

"Okay, calm the fuck down! This Adam? Is he the man who destroyed half my bar and ruined my mother's birthday cake that *you* decorated? The man you said is your husband? This is the same man you want me to help?"

"I'm so sorry about all that, Jep, I am, but we need to help him. I can't do it on my own. The house—it's not safe anymore."

Jepson frowned and covered his face, raking his hands through his hair. "I need you to show me where this house is."

"You're just going to kill him, aren't you?" Her voice was small and meek.

"No," he answered, defeated. "We're going to save him."

"And you'll do this for me?" she asked. "You won't hurt him?"

"Do you want my help or not?" Jepson gestured for Olive to lead the way. "Where are we headed?"

She stopped short, turning back. "I thought you said I was crazy. You just told me I needed help. Now you're all of a sudden so eager to have me lead the way to my husband, who you say is a beast? How do I know I can trust you?"

He looked down at his feet, shifting. "Because you're asking me for help, and I'm not sure how or why, but you've become a fast friend of mine. What other answer do you need?"

Olive huffed and continued towards the house, panting and stomping as she spoke. "Why are you friends with me? I thought you were coming onto me at first, but I know now that wasn't it. You like to befriend people who aren't in the best of ways, but why?"

"Because I know what it's like to feel judged, okay?" he whispered through clenched teeth, following her. "Why does it matter?"

"Jepson, I have no choice but to hope I can trust you. But I don't even know you! You think you can just walk up to anyone and be friends with them? That's what you did to me, and it worked, but now I find myself trusting you with saving Adam, even though you already said you want to kill him."

"So, what do you want from me, Basketcase? You say you can't trust me and then you say you have no choice but to trust me." Jepson sighed. "You said the house is falling down, and we're wasting time going around in circles not accomplishing anything."

As they grew closer and closer to the house, Olive realized that wasting time was exactly what she was doing. The thought of going back scared her, both because of how dangerous the house was and how violent Adam was, too. Part of her wanted to save him, but part of her wanted him to suffer.

She looked in the direction of where the house was, just beyond the brush ahead of them, and took a deep, worried sigh. She stopped walking and turned back to Jepson, unable to reason with herself and move forward.

"You approached me because I was having a tantrum in the mud and yelling about things that couldn't possibly be true," Olive continued, stalling again. "You wanted to be someone who could help, but what happens when you find out that all of this wasn't just in my head?

"What is all of this?" he sneered. "Look, I'm sorry I didn't come onto you, if that's what you were expecting from me, but you're not even my type. I prefer—blonde women."

"What!" she screeched. "How can you think this is what this is about? I'm a married woman, and you don't even *like* women in that way!"

Jepson's frustrated expression switched to contempt. His eyes narrowed, and he gritted his teeth at her. "You really are a basket-case, aren't you?" he said, looking her up and down.

"That's what they say." She clicked her tongue and rolled her eyes again. "And by 'they,' I mean you, because you've said that exact thing to me before! Why do you have to keep telling me I'm crazy? Is that all you think I am? Just some child who needs your help?"

She inched closer and closer to him with each word, her voice growing louder and angrier with each step. "Does it make you feel better about yourself to tell yourself you're helping a woman who's gone mad? Are you covering for your own insecurities? Can't you just be forward with yourself? If you had had the common decency to listen to me instead of shutting down every word I've told you, then you'd know the hell I've been through! Now help me, dammit! Help me! *Help me! HELP ME!*"

Jepson backed away from her with wide eyes. He tripped and fell onto a rock behind him and onto his backside. Scrambling to stand again, he pointed a finger back at her and shouted: "You stay away from me, Basketcase. There's something wrong with you, you know that? You and that thing you call your husband, you shouldn't exist. Stay away from me, and stay out of Sidney, or I'll—I'll have you both thrown in the loony bin!"

CHAPTER 18
Acting Alone

Olive stood slouched and silent as Jepson ran back towards the town. Guilt hung in the air around her as she realized she'd scared away her only friend. She remembered how Rose had been afraid of her, too, and how her own brother and father hadn't remembered her. Worst of all, her husband was too dangerous to be around.

Olive felt hopeless and very alone, which diminished what little desire she still had left to move forward. Having no ambition, no optimism, and no direction, Olive fell to her knees and stared blankly in the direction of the brush, and at what she could see of the house beyond it. Though at a distance it appeared intact from the outside, she could still hear the inner walls of the house whining and moaning.

It was in that moment of hopeless despair, looking up at the withered, ugly house that was even uglier and more disgusting on the inside, that Olive realized once again how foolish she had been about Adam all along. Adam wasn't a good man, as she'd claimed him to be. He had always looked down on people and been cruel to those he saw as inferior. He had only ever worked hard at something if and when he wanted to do so. He'd relied on his servants, and on Olive, to take care of his cooking, cleaning and other basic needs.

Olive gritted her teeth thinking about it all. She thought about all the hard work her family put into their businesses, and remembered why she'd never wanted to be royalty in the first place.

A lifetime of living well, without being expected to put forth effort, had caused Adam to feel entitled. Required to provide for himself, he'd stolen from the townspeople and destroyed their property. He'd killed livestock and pets, causing the people of Sidney to grieve and fear their surroundings.

Olive clenched her jaw until it ached. Her eyes narrowed, even though there was no one around to see her glower.

Adam had no remorse for the heartbreak he'd caused others, nor did he feel guilty for the times he'd hurt Olive. He'd dismissed it all by blaming the harm on her, imprisoning her, and lying to her over and over again.

Olive's anger had reached a point where it made her feel queasy and weak. She no longer heard hissing between her ears or gained energy from the feeling. Instead, it drained her, the same as it always had in the past. Her teeth felt sore as she released the tension in her jaw, and the feelings of fury fell from the tight place in her chest downwards into a dead lump in the bottom of her stomach. She felt sad, tired, hungry, and very alone.

Olive lay on her side in the grass and dirt, curling her legs against her chest. She didn't want to try anymore. She didn't want to turn back time, either. She had given it her all and tried her best, but the whole thing had come crashing down anyway. Maybe Adam had been right. Maybe they were doomed, she decided as she welcomed new tears. Perhaps they *were* in Hell, and deserved whatever was coming to them.

A hum droned in her ears as she wept, but she did nothing to stop. It whirred on and became louder until she thought she could hear voices along with it.

She sat up to focus on the voices, which grew louder and clearer as she wiped her tears away. The sounds weren't inside her head, she realized; they were coming from the town, and it sounded like they were singing.

Olive looked towards the town to find a large group of people moving in her direction. Some of them were carrying lanterns, and many of them were singing or chanting in loud and rambunctious tones. She sat still and listened so she could make out their words:

"Kill the beast—*kill the beast—kill the beast!*"

Olive gasped, scrambling towards the house through the tall grass and brush, staying low on her hands and feet so that no one could see her. Twigs and thorns tore at her dress, as well as her arm and the back of her hand. She was through most of the thicker brush when she decided to stand and sprint towards the house. As the mob drew closer, Olive could see that the lanterns she'd thought they'd been carrying were lit torches, which they were using to burn through the brush in their way.

Olive reached the double front doors of the house, ahead of the mob, standing her ground and blocking them from entering.

"NO!" she screamed at the mob as they reached the house. "He's a good man! He's kind and sweet and gentle!"

Olive didn't believe her own words, but part of her still loved Adam enough to protect him from harm. She had little strength left to fight for him, but she wouldn't let him die with such indignity.

She scanned the mob but saw no sign of Jepson. The townspeople continued chanting, bypassing her as they shoved toward the doors. Some pushed her back and forth to get through the doorway, while others piled in and around the house through broken windows.

Olive slipped into the woods that bordered the sides of the property, hoping to find that Adam had already escaped. She wasn't sure why she wanted to see him, or what she'd say to him when she did, but she wanted to get to him before the mob did.

She found no sign of him in the woods, nor any fresh footprints, scraps of clothing, or otherwise. Several members of the mob had followed her, leading her to circle back towards the house. She considered finding a way back inside to search for Adam there, but she knew the dangers of entering the unstable structure were made worse by the mob tramping through it.

She reached the back of the house, where large glass windows peered into the kitchen Adam had built for her. The windows were shielded by layers of unkempt trellises crawling with overgrown roses and ivy. Olive scanned the windows for a clear opening or broken window where she could climb the trellises to see inside.

That's when she spotted Adam. He was difficult to view from the ground where she stood, but through a small, empty patch of dead roses in a clouded side window of the kitchen, she could see upwards and through to one of the skylights above. A familiar brown shadow was moving at a sluggish pace along the roof.

The men in the mob were either searching the woods or inside the house, leaving Olive confident she'd be able to scale the back of the house undetected. She pulled the top layer of her skirt over the back of her head like a hood, hoping it would help her fit in with the rest of the mob, most of whom were wearing heavy coats with hats or hoods.

The weather had warmed since that morning, and the snowflakes had melted into a cold, wet layer glazing the grass and brush. The sky threatened a storm, delivering a sporadic sprinkling of rain and quiet, rolling thunder. Olive cleared away as much of the leaves and ivy as she could from the trellis that bordered the kitchen window, using it to climb towards where she'd seen Adam. Slimy leaves and dried flower petals stuck to her hands and arms as she scaled each rung, and age-old thorns pierced her fingers, but she barely noticed as she continued climbing.

Fat raindrops were born from the thunder and drizzle, falling atop her head and back as she finally reached the roof. Adam was still where she'd seen him before, unclothed and covered in thick brown fur. He lay on his side along the skylight above the kitchen, motionless aside from his labored breathing. Olive muffled a sob and crawled toward him. The rain turned heavy, which made the steep incline of the slippery glass roof even more dangerous. The house moaned and creaked as the mob pillaged the rooms inside. The kitchen wing underneath them, however, still remained unscathed.

"Adam," she whispered.

He lay with his back to her.

"Adam, look at me."

"Go away. You deserve better than all this. Just let me die here. Please." He pleaded, but he sounded empty and numb.

"Sweetheart, listen to me." Olive whispered, her words sounding forced and unconvincing. "You can run away. You can find your own island, maybe, or a secluded place in the woods. You can learn from this. I know you can."

When she was close enough to him, she grasped his furry shoulder and lay him flat against the skylight so she could see his face. His head, face, neck, and shoulders were sheathed in fur and thick brown whiskers.

"Why do you hate me, Olive?" Adam spoke in a shallow voice, still refusing to look at her.

She swept aside a lock of long fur from his eyes. "I don't hate you, Adam. I'm just disappointed in you."

A growl rumbled from his throat. "Then why do *they* hate me?" He sat up and pointed towards the front of the house, his voice dark and deep.

The mob's chanting still hummed in the air. Olive wiped a handful of tears into the rain and regained her will to let Adam go. She knew the answer to his question, and she knew neither of them would like it if she spoke it aloud.

"They hate you because—" she took a deep breath and held her head high—"they're not as stupid as I am."

Adam growled again, this time in a way that shook the roof and bellowed through the air. The vibrations sent Olive sliding back down the steep angle of the glass skylight towards the base of the rooftop. She didn't move toward the trellis again, but instead watched Adam. Beams of light poured outward from his sharp teeth and large, claw-like hands. The light shot into the dark blue sky above, dancing with the scattered clouds. Stars of every color trickled down, mingling with the trails of light.

The skylight underneath Adam shattered, sending him falling onto the center island in the kitchen below. Olive could still see him through the glass, lying motionless inside the room he'd built for her.

She sidled down the rose trellis to find that the mob had finally stopped their chanting and madness. Instead, everyone was watching the light show in the sky.

"There's a man in the house who's hurt!" Olive yelled. "He's going to die if we don't help him!"

Her voice had been loud enough, yet no one turned to her. The mob was stone-focused on the sky above, which continued to dance and play with brilliant light.

"Listen to me, please! One of the men. One of *your* men fell into the house and is hurt!" Her voice was frantic and high-pitched. It cracked and broke as she yelled into the rainy night.

"Are you all deaf? Do you not hear this woman is speaking to you?"

Jepson's deep voice echoed loud and clear from behind her. The men turned their attention away from the sky at the sound of his voice.

"Where the hell have you been?" Olive shouted to Jepson as he approached.

"I chickened out, okay? I ran off." He whispered so that only she could hear.

"You chickened out of your own mob?" she hissed back.

"Shhh—!" He looked at her with wide eyes, then back at the mob. "Listen, men! There is a man inside this house who needs our help! Olive here knows where he is, so let us follow her lead."

She glared at Jepson and headed around the front of the house. He stayed at her side.

"How do you just abandon your own mob?" She was quiet, but spoke with an edge as they walked.

"Think before you speak!" he hissed, shushing her again. "I'm trying to direct a mob here."

"*Now* you take control of them? You're a piece of work, you know that, Jep?"

"You know, Basketcase," he whispered again, "despite my gorgeous face and solid physique, I'm not always perfect, alright? I realized I was making a big mistake as I led them all up here, but it was already out of my control by then.”

They'd reached the front of the house, which no longer had a front door or even a front wall. The mob had leveled the entire front half of the house. All that remained intact were pieces of the sitting room and the back two wings.

“I'm sorry, Olive,” Jepson told her, frowning at the pile of rubble in front of them.

“Did you just call me Olive?” she sneered.

“I did.”

“Stop doing that.”

He rolled his eyes. “Please, just lead the way, Basketcase.”

“That back room to the right!” She directed the mob towards the kitchen as they stood in the archway between the two wings. “I don't even know if we can get through, though. There's too much rubble in the hallway.”

“Men, clear away this mess,” Jepson ordered the crowd. “The man who needs our help is in the room at the end of this hallway.”

“The man inside that room is Adam.” Olive whispered to Jepson.

“Yes, I gathered that,” he said. “I told you we'd help him, and we will.”

“No, you don't understand. The *man* inside that room is my husband.” She looked gravely into Jepson's eyes as the crowd managed to open the kitchen door.

Adam lay tan-skinned, naked, and lifeless upon the kitchen island. A spattering of short dark hair graced the top of his head, his chest, stomach, and his nether regions. His mouth was open in anguish, displaying five of his front teeth, all of which were even and white and no longer fang-like.

Two men from the crowd approached Adam and checked his arms and neck for a pulse.

"This man is dead, sir," one of them said to Jepson.

Olive gasped, and Jepson sighed.

"Check him again," he ordered.

The two men continued to search for a pulse while Jepson approached the table. He held his hand above Adam's mouth and placed an ear against his chest, shaking his head.

Silence fell over the house for a moment. Jepson looked back at Olive, lowering his head and closing his eyes. Adam was gone, but somehow Olive realized that she'd known that already. She sighed and began to cry, feeling as much sadness as relief.

CHAPTER 19
Family

The mob had cleared, but Olive stayed in the kitchen. She had nowhere else she wanted to go, despite Jepson offering to let her stay in the House of Counsel. Jepson had planned to send a burial team the following day, but the thought of leaving Adam's body alone inside the house overnight spooked Olive. He had been a bad man, she knew that, but he was her family, her rock, and the only one who'd still known her after the supermoon. Even after everything she'd accomplished, without Adam, Olive had nothing and no one to call home.

It was dark and cold, and the ground was still wet from the rain. Olive sat against a tree outside, staring at the house and finally allowing herself to wallow in what felt like a confusing and senseless fate. She had wrapped herself in a pair of heavy, dusty curtains she'd snagged on the way out.

"Deserves a proper cremation," came a man's voice behind her.

Olive looked around the tree trunk to see a small, dark figure approaching with soft footsteps.

"Lionel?" she asked. "What are you doing here?"

"We're going to get rid of all this." He gestured at the house. "You and me, sis."

Olive gasped and laughed all at once. "So, you—?"

He held up a hand to stop her. "I have no memories—at all—of you before a few days back. I don't remember us being kids together, or anything about your wedding, and I don't remember you managing the bakery. As far as I can recall, none of that happened."

Olive's gaze fell. "Oh," she said, deflated.

Lionel held a finger to his temple, tapping a few times before speaking again. "What I do remember, though—is *you*. Your mannerisms, your voice, the ridiculous way you dance. I was even able to predict your sense of humor from the end of our first *very strange* conversation. I don't know what that is, but I can't keep pretending it's nothing."

Olive let out an exasperated laugh, followed by tears. "It's because we're family!"

Lionel nodded. His lips were closed and still, but he smiled with his eyes. Olive stood, rushing to meet her brother with a hug. She knew he hated hugs, even from her, but he accepted the embrace and returned it before reminding her why he'd come to meet her.

"Can we burn this piece of shit to the ground now, please?" Lionel pulled a box of matches and 2 large bottles of brandy from his coat pocket, gesturing towards the house. "I don't know whether to respect it on your behalf—or hate it out of respect for you, but we can't let it sit here and rot."

"Are you talking about the house? Or—?" Olive asked.

"Both." They answered together.

Discarded torches had been littered around the outside of the house, which they relit to help see their way and disperse the fire where it needed to be. What remained of the house was damp, but the brandy helped to keep the flames going. They worked together throughout the night, finding dry twigs underneath wet brush to feed to the fire, which continued to stay small and controlled due to the damp ground and wood.

Daylight was on the horizon when the door to the kitchen took flame. The kitchen was the last unburned piece of the house, and the one they'd been avoiding.

"Let's go." Olive said, afraid that she'd be able to see Adam's body inside the kitchen once the door burned through.

Lionel sighed. "You know we can't do that, Olive."

Olive scoffed. "But it's aflame already, and it's about to rain again. It'll burn over like it's supposed to, and then the rain will put it out."

Lionel sighed again. "Do you remember when we put out the oven flames and left all the bread inside while we left to visit a friend? You were adamant that as long as we kept the oven door closed, it would keep the heat inside long enough for the bread to finish baking."

"Of course. I do that all the time," Olive agreed.

"And what happened?" he urged. "Think back, Olive. It was a very warm summer day. I was probably about fifteen at the time."

"We burned it." Olive beamed. "The oven didn't cool fast enough because the weather was too hot. We burned all the bread for the next day and had to wake up before dawn to rebake it all."

"Mmm-hmm." He nodded. "We're not doing that here. Too dangerous."

"Lionel?"

"Yes?"

"What else do you remember?" she asked, still smiling at him.

He looked back towards her, grinning at the realization, too. The two siblings erupted with immediate laughter.

"Brother!" she shouted into the sky above.

"Sister!" he responded, mimicking her.

A loud clap of thunder interrupted them, followed by a bolt of lightning so close they could feel the static in the air around them. The low, controlled flame they'd created from the kitchen door grew, encircling the rest of the room and rising higher to engulf the ceiling.

Olive and Lionel stepped back, surveying the fire but keeping a safe distance. Despite the display, the flames stayed confined to the area where the kitchen had once stood, leaving the trees and brush around it unscathed.

They sat cross-legged on the damp ground, watching and waiting as exhaustion set in from the night of hard labor and no sleep. Lionel rested his back against a tree and began nodding off. Olive yawned and rubbed her eyes. As she did, she saw something move behind the flames.

She rubbed her eyes again and looked over at Lionel, who was half-asleep.

Olive stood and tiptoed closer to the figure she'd seen moving. "Adam?" she whispered.

The figure moved again, rustling twigs and brush in its way. Its actions were erratic, as if it wanted to be noticed and followed, so Olive continued to follow it around the circle of fire still burning through the kitchen. The figure was not Adam, she realized. It was smaller and appeared to have features much lighter in color. Its steps were dainty and playful, too, not heavy and slow like Adam's had been. She had nearly reached the side of the flame wall that bordered the woods when the figure changed course. Olive caught a glimpse of long blonde hair as they darted off, disappearing into the woods.

Thunder clapped again then, and the sky opened up, releasing sheets of rain that extinguished the fire within minutes. Olive returned to Lionel's side, and they watched as the smoke cleared, revealing that the demolition was complete. Rain pummeled the piles of ash, allowing it to mix with the dirt below, and the smell of petrichor clouded the smell of burning wood.

All that remained were cracked and broken slabs of marble and other stones, an eerie but beautiful reminder that something grand had once stood there.

CHAPTER 20
Just the Beginning
One Month Later

Once upon a chilly autumn afternoon, a crisp layer of sparkling snow fell over the Land of Sidney. The air smelled of fresh-baked pumpkin bread, and children danced with each other in the town commons, singing Christmas carols in anticipation of the upcoming holidays.

Olive closed up shop early at Grimm's Bakery. She wrapped two large loaves of pumpkin bread and placed them into a covered basket, whistling to herself and sporting a dark red cloak with a cozy hood. She strolled towards the commons, the basket of gifts swinging from one arm.

"'Ey, Basketcase! We don't have to be there for at least an hour." Jepson sat cross-legged against the side of a small fountain in the center of the commons.

"It's a belated birthday party, Jepson." She smiled. "I'm sure your mother won't mind if we're there a little early, considering you weren't there at all on her actual birthday."

"And whose fault was that? I got fired from cake duty because of you."

"Then here: give her this for me. Say it's from you. It'll help you get back on her good side." Olive handed Jepson the basket of pumpkin bread and plopped down next to him on the side of the fountain. "Anyway,

I was hoping you'd be here, too. So much has happened since we last saw each other."

"The house burned down, didn't it?" Jepson asked. "Lightning, I heard. I'm sorry to hear."

Olive glanced at him sideways. "It was better that way. A proper cremation."

"He was a bad person. You know that, right?" Jepson's eyes narrowed.

She looked down at her feet. "Yes. I know that better than anyone."

Jepson frowned. "Well, I'll bet you're glad it's all over and done with now."

"All done and over with?" Olive clicked her tongue. "When I was a little girl, I was made to believe that getting married was to be a grand and happy ending. Although, 'ending' means something is done and over, even though it doesn't really end at all. I had my storybook happily-ever-after, but it was only the beginning."

"That's not what I meant, Bask—"

"And it's not over now either. I've been through so much, but still, nothing is ending! Are you following, Jep?"

He smiled, shaking his head. "Well, something must have ended, because Lionel remembers you again. He said he always sort of did. What's the story with that?"

Olive's voice lifted. "Sometimes things get twisted, Jep, and sometimes it needs to be that way for a while. My family remembers me, too. They acted like they'd never forgotten me at all. Same with everyone else I knew before."

"Do they remember you becoming a royal princess, too?" Jepson teased. "Do you still think you married a prince and moved into a palace?"

"What I remember and what others remember are not the same thing, and that's just part of my story." Olive smirked. "Everyone is living their own experience. But if you must know, everyone thinks I ran away with the woodsmith's estranged son."

"And that's not what happened?" He smirked back.

She looked at him sideways. "It's not your story. It's mine."

He shrugged. "Fair enough."

"It's my story, and I'm taking control of it." Olive beamed. "I'm leaving Sidney, Jep."

"Leaving?" he asked, surprised. "When?"

She stared up at the falling snow. "Whenever I'm ready. I want to be something more than a baker or a wife. There must be more to life than *this.*" She crinkled her nose as she looked around the common area.

"What's so bad about Sidney?" he asked.

"It's not bad, just… *provincial.*" Olive continued. "It's ordinary. I've been through things I can't explain, some of it beautiful and some of it so, so awful. All I know is that I don't think I'm meant to stay put anymore. I feel so out of place now. I'm a *widow*, Jep, and everyone knows it! If I really wanted my story to end, I could just stay in Sidney where I'd be doomed for a dull and disappointing existence."

"I think I'm starting to understand now." Jepson chuckled. "I still think you're a basket-case, though."

"Although I am looking forward to living with my brothers for the winter season. It will be nice to relax and spend some time with them before I go. Lionel and I are planning to bake 1000 Christmas cookies to give as gifts around town. We always talked about doing that when we were kids."

Jepson raised an eyebrow at her. "So, you're living with Lionel?"

"For a bit, yes." She nodded. "I'll be keeping house for us all until winter has passed, when travel is safer again."

"Ain't that just the weirdest thing." Jepson smiled, giddy with excitement.

"What's weird about it?"

"He asked me to live with him, too." Jepson's face flushed.

Olive cackled. "I knew it! You and Lionel?"

He nodded, covering half of his face.-

"That's so exciting, Jep. I always knew Lionel was different, too. He never played much with the rest of my brothers. It was more like Lionel and I were the best of friends, and the others had their own group. We'd bake cookies and play with dolls—he'd even do my hair sometimes! Lionel's the best sister I never had."

"He's a pretty good beau, too," Jepson whispered, flashing a toothy smile at her.

"I like that." She smiled back. "Although, won't people start asking questions if the two of you are living together? Do you think the town will be tolerant of it?"

"No." He shook his head. "A place like Sidney will not approve. I sometimes wish things were different like that. I wish we could live in a world where people like me aren't looked down on. Where we can live in a way that makes us happy. It's not like we're hurting anyone."

Olive thought back to a conversation she'd had with Rose before her wedding, where Rose had expressed how she wanted the world to be different. Rose had wanted a world where people had a chance to be great no matter what type of family they were born into—no matter how strange or poor they were. This new world, Olive realized, was exactly that.

"Hmm," Olive thought aloud.

"What is it?" Jepson asked.

"I agree with you, Jep. And there's someone we should find who might be able to help."

"Okay." He shrugged. "Who is this person?"

"Also." She ignored him. "I don't know what's about to happen, but if this doesn't work the way I want it to, you and I can pretend to be married for a few months until I leave Sidney. Then, once I leave, we can just say that I split up the marriage. That way, it'll still just seem like you're living with family. People have already seen us gallivanting around town together, so it's perfect."

"You're all over the place, Basketcase, but that's not a half-bad idea. I think it'll be pretty fun living with you and Lionel."

"About that. I said I live with my *brothers*, not brother. I have six of them," she added.

Jepson's eyes widened.

"Of course Lionel didn't tell you." She shook her head. "I'd expect that's the first thing you'd want to know. That's so like him, though. He's shy, you know that, but he also tends to keep embarrassing information bottled up because he's embarrassed to talk about them, even when it's the *most* important thing." Olive huffed and looked down at her feet. "Six brothers and myself, in one house, and not a one of us are married. Welcome to the Grimm's Bachelor Hut. We're a weird, workaholic restaurant family. Some may even say we're wicked. All my brothers are quirkier than I am, and I guess they just haven't found their special somebodies yet. I think maybe they feel like they'll never be alone as long as they have each other."

"That's pretty grim, Basketcase," Jepson joked.

"Oh, you're so funny," she joked back. "Lionel is as shy as can be! He never likes to talk to anyone except me when we're working together, which is difficult with restaurant work. And our brother, Sam, is always sick! Even when he's not sick, he thinks he is, so he does all the book-keeping so he doesn't have to work with food. But Joe is the weirdest of them all! He gets up before dawn every morning and goes to work in the deli. He cuts all the meat and cheese, and then he cleans the whole deli, top to bottom, until it's spotless. Then he's done for the day by lunchtime so he can go back to bed and do the whole thing over again the next day."

"Wait," Jepson asked. "So, your brother Joe goes to sleep at lunchtime and then sleeps until the next morning? And he does this every day?"

She nodded. "I told you. They're interesting characters. I told him that maybe he should start doing lunch dates before he goes to bed. Maybe he'll find some sleepy girl who wants to take naps with him for the rest of forever."

"You're peculiar, Basketcase."

"No, Joe's the peculiar one," she teased.

"It sounds like Joe is the sleepy one, Sam is the sniffly one, and Lionel is the shy one. I still say you're the peculiar one."

"Oh, and then this other brother I have is such an annoying know-it-all. He wants to hang out with me all the time and tell me I'm wrong about *everything*."

"Who's that one?" Jepson asked. "I'll make sure to watch out for him."

"His name is Jepson—"

"Ouch. That hurt, Basketcase," he joked. "So if I'm your brother, too, then that makes seven of us."

"And I'm about to be stuck living with all seven of you for a while!" Olive said in a fake snotty tone. "I feel another adventure right around the corner."

"Speaking of that," Jepson started. "What were you babbling on about before? You needed to find someone who could help with—something."

At that exact moment, Olive looked out over the commons to see a familiar face looking back in her direction. It was Rose, but she looked much different than Olive remembered her. Instead of the meek, uncomfortable demeanor she'd held in the palace, Rose stood straight and tall. Her blonde hair was pulled back into a neat braid that she wrapped around one of her shoulders. She wore a confident smile and a gorgeous blue cloak.

Rose nodded at Olive and bowed her head. Olive did the same. The two women locked stares from across the commons.

"Do you know Rose?" Jepson asked.

"I do," Olive answered. "She's sort of an old friend."

"Rose is my mother's tailor. Very talented girl," he started. "She'll be at the party tonight. You two should catch up."

Olive smiled. "She said she always dreamed of wearing something blue like that."

"Uh-oh, Basketcase. Do you like girls?"

"No," Olive said, smirking. "But I think Rose might be the one to help us."

"Are you sewing something?"

"Never mind, Jep. I'll loop you back in later." She patted his shoulder.

"No one ever has any idea what you're talking about, Basketcase."

"Good." Olive smirked.

"Word around the House of Counsel is that Rose got an offer to make a dress for a princess in India. A real princess—not like you, Basketcase."

Olive gasped with excitement. "I've been hearing customers talk about that princess. She's not in India, though. I thought it was somewhere else. Somewhere that starts with an A. Agra-something."

"Hmm." He nodded. "That sounds right. Are you ready to head over to Mom's party?"

She jumped up. "Let's go! I'm excited to meet everyone!"

He stood and bent his elbow as if to invite Olive to link arms with him, but instead hooked his gigantic arm around her neck, holding her in a playful headlock as they headed towards the House of Counsel.

"You're coming with me, fake wife," he teased.

Olive half-struggled to free herself from Jepson's hold. "I'm not your fake wife yet, and right now you are my least favorite fake brother."

"Yeah, but I'm the only fake brother you've got."

"Thanks, Doc Know-It-All."

"You're welcome, Basketcase."

FIN

ABOUT THE AUTHOR

Sarah J Antoinette was born and raised in Chicago, Illinois. She has been writing independent books and stories since she first learned to read and write at the age of six. After moving to Denver and ending a long-term, abusive relationship in her mid-twenties, Sarah began a semi-successful string of online blogs tracking her emotional recovery. One of the blogs featured a series of short semi-autobiographical fractured fairy tales, many of which she plans to write into full length novels.

Basketcase, A Classic Tale in Reverse is Sarah's first full length, published novel. She. The book was originally published in 2016 and then re-released in 2020 under a second edition.

Sarah hopes to continue writing novels that focus on empowering women to be unique, independent, and intelligent.

www.ingramcontent.com/pod-product-compliance
Lightning Source LLC
Chambersburg PA
CBHW032034050726
47590CB00006B/2399